Off Broadway Festival

40th Series

Blind
by Gloria Calderon Kellett

Evelyn Shaffer and the Chance of a Lifetime
by Greg Edwards and Andy Roninson

The Gulf
Audrey Cefaly

Narrators
by Simon Henriques

Seabird Is in a Happy Place
by James Gordon King

Throws of Love
by Amy Staats

A SAMUEL FRENCH ACTING EDITION

FOUNDED 1830

SAMUELFRENCH.COM
SAMUELFRENCH-LONDON.CO.UK

BLIND Copyright © 2015 by Gloria Calderon Kellett
EVELYN SHAFFER AND THE CHANCE OF A LIFETIME Copyright © 2015 by Greg Edwards & Andy Roninson
THE GULF Copyright © 2015 by Audrey Cefaly
NARRATORS Copyright © 2015 by Simon Henriques
SEABIRD IS IN A HAPPY PLACE Copyright © 2015 by James Gordon King
THROWS OF LOVE Copyright © 2015 by Amy Staats

All Rights Reserved

All titles in this collection *(BLIND, EVELYN SHAFFER AND THE CHANCE OF A LIFETIME, THE GULF, NARRATORS, SEABIRD IS IN A HAPPY PLACE, THROWS OF LOVE)* fully protected under the copyright laws of the United States of America, the British Commonwealth, including Canada, and all other countries of the Copyright Union. All rights, including professional and amateur stage productions, recitation, lecturing, public reading, motion picture, radio broadcasting, television and the rights of translation into foreign languages are strictly reserved.

ISBN 978-0-573-70480-2

www.samuelfrench.com
www.SamuelFrench-London.co.uk

FOR PRODUCTION ENQUIRIES

UNITED STATES AND CANADA
Info@Samuelfrench.com
1-866-598-8449

UNITED KINGDOM AND EUROPE
Plays@SamuelFrench-London.co.uk
020-7255-4302

Each title is subject to availability from Samuel French, depending upon country of performance. Please be aware that *BLIND, EVELYN SHAFFER AND THE CHANCE OF A LIFETIME, THE GULF, NARRATORS, SEABIRD IS IN A HAPPY PLACE*, and/or *THROWS OF LOVE* may not be licensed by Samuel French in your territory. Professional and amateur producers should contact the nearest Samuel French office or licensing partner to verify availability.

CAUTION: Professional and amateur producers are hereby warned that *BLIND, EVELYN SHAFFER AND THE CHANCE OF A LIFETIME, THE GULF, NARRATORS, SEABIRD IS IN A HAPPY PLACE,* and/or *THROWS OF LOVE* is/are subject to a licensing fee. Publication of this play(s) does not imply availability for performance. Both amateurs and professionals considering a production are strongly advised to apply to Samuel French before starting rehearsals, advertising, or booking a theatre. A licensing fee must be paid whether the title(s) is presented for charity or gain and whether or not admission is charged. Professional/Stock licensing fees are quoted upon application to Samuel French.

No one shall make any changes in this title(s) for the purpose of production. No part of this book may be reproduced, stored in a retrieval system, or transmitted in any form, by any means, now known or yet to be invented, including mechanical, electronic, photocopying, recording, videotaping, or otherwise, without the prior written permission of the publisher. No one shall upload this title(s), or part of this title(s), to any social media websites.

For all enquiries regarding motion picture, television, and other media rights, please contact Samuel French.

MUSIC USE NOTE

Licensees are solely responsible for obtaining formal written permission from copyright owners to use copyrighted music in the performance of this play and are strongly cautioned to do so. If no such permission is obtained by the licensee, then the licensee must use only original music that the licensee owns and controls. Licensees are solely responsible and liable for all music clearances and shall indemnify the copyright owners of the play(s) and their licensing agent, Samuel French, against any costs, expenses, losses and liabilities arising from the use of music by licensees. Please contact the appropriate music licensing authority in your territory for the rights to any incidental music.

IMPORTANT BILLING AND CREDIT REQUIREMENTS

If you have obtained performance rights to this title, please refer to your licensing agreement for important billing and credit requirements.

The Samuel French Off Off Broadway Short Play Festival started in 1975 and is one of the nation's most established and highly regarded short play festivals. During the course of the Festival's 40 years, more than 500 theatre companies and schools participated in the Festival, including companies from coast to coast as well as abroad from Canada, Singapore, and the United Kingdom. Over the years, more than 200 submitted plays have been published, with many of the participants becoming established, award-winning playwrights.

Festival Co-Artistic Directors: Amy Rose Marsh and Casey McLain
Literary Coordinator: Ben Coleman
Judge Coordinator: Abbie Van Nostrand
Marketing Team: Chris Kam, Courtney Kochuba, Ryan Pointer
Abbie Van Nostrand
Press: Keith Sherman and Associates
Stage Manager: Laura Manos-Hey
Assistant Stage Manager: Cara Kramer
House Manager: Tyler Mullen
President: Nate Collins
Executive Director: Bruce Lazarus
Director of Operations: Ken Dingledine
Festival Coordinators: Coryn Carson, Elizabeth Minski
Festival Interns: Marissa Arellano, Alexa Derman, Brandon Mancuso
Festival Staff: Christian Amato, Caitlin Bartow, Jennifer Carter, Nick Dawson, Julia Izumi, David Kimple, Ryan McLeod, Ashley Moniz, Jonah Rosen, Becca Schlossberg, Emily Sorensen, Sarah Weber

FESTIVAL KEYNOTE SPEAKER
Theresa Rebeck

GUEST JUDGES
Nan Barnett
Sharon Fallon
Matthew Freeman
Jeff Griffin
Dennis Gromelski
Abigail Katz
Laura Penn
Heidi Schreck
Adam Szymkowicz
Paul Thureen
Susan Westfall
Lauren Yee

For more information on the Samuel French Off Off Broadway Short Play Festival, including history, interviews, and more, please visit www.oob.samuelfrench.com.

FOREWORD

Last year was a milestone year for the Samuel French Off Off Broadway Short Play Festival: Year Forty. The Festival started in 1975, before the Actor's Theatre of Louisville's famous Humana New Play Festival, before South Coast Repertory Theatre introduced the Pacific Playwrights, and before Miami's City Theatre – the only professional theatre in the United State dedicated exclusively to the short play form – started producing their "Summer Shorts" series. It was a truly groundbreaking event.

The Festival had humble roots. Back in 1975, the Managing Editor of Samuel French, Bill Talbott, started a play "competition" in order to form deeper connections with emerging writers, which would become the Samuel French Festival. In the first four years, only one to three playwrights were declared "winners." The plays were read, produced in a showcase production in New York, and winning plays received a publication and licensing contract with Samuel French. The talent pool was so rich, however, that the Festival quickly expanded, growing to eight winners, and finally settling on six writers. Many of these winning writers have gone on to have notable careers as professional playwrights and television showrunners.

Today, the festival not only functions as a launch pad for major playwrights, but also as a labor of love on the part of the employees of Samuel French and a celebration of grassroots theatre-making. Our staff, who mans the phones and desks of the office by day, donate time, effort, and energy to the Festival at night. Submissions for the Festival number well over 1400; each play is read at least two times by volunteer employees who passionately advocate for their favorites. During our week of performances, all production elements are designed, planned, and managed by French staff, many of who have pasts as professional theatre practitioners. The donation of time on the part of our staff – and is it a lot of time to mount a festival! – is a true testament to Samuel French's continued dedication to the playwright.

That said, we are very excited to present our fortieth collection of short plays, selected by the Samuel French staff as well as many notable members of the theatre community who worked as our judges. Featuring a vast range of styles and stories, this year, we are also celebrating the Festival's first short musical. We are proud of this collection, humbled by the talents of these writers, and honored to be a part of Samuel French's mission: to champion the work of playwrights. We hope you feel the same way.

Happy play-reading.

Amy Rose Marsh and Casey McLain
Co-Artistic Directors
The Samuel French Off Off Broadway Short Play Festival Festival

FESTIVAL PARTICIPANTS
- THE TOP 30 –
AT THE FINISH by Nick Gandiello
BERMUDA BLUE by Ross Dunsmore
BILLY BITCHASS by Ira Gamerman
BLIND by Gloria Calderon Kellett
A BRIEF HISTORY OF AMERICA by Dipika Guha
THE BRIGHTER THE STAR by Katharine Henner
THE CHECKER GAME by Steve Warren
THE CROCODILE'S BITE by Vanessa Garcia
EIGHT SECONDS by Sean Harris Oliver
EVELYN SHAFFER AND THE CHANCE OF A LIFETIME by Greg Edwards &
Andy Roninson
GAY FOR PAY by Benjamin Scuglia
GINNY by Anna Fox
GLAMPING by Carey Crim
THE GULF by Audrey Cefaly
HAPPY ANNIVERSARY by Charly E. Simpson
LUCKY NUMBERS by Gwendolyn Rice
MAKE JOHN PATRICK SHANLEY GO HOME by Holli Harms
THE MALTESE WALTER by John Minigan
NARRATORS by Simon Henriques
NATURALISTIC COMMERCIALS by Ben Vigus
THE OFFER by Bella Poynton
THROWS OF LOVE by Amy Staats
SALT by Peter Turo
THE SALTY PART OF THE ANIMAL by Erin Mallon
SEABIRD IS IN A HAPPY PLACE by James Gordon King
SO YOU'RE HER by Arnold Shelby
TASTES LIKE TEEN SPIRIT! By Sara Israel
THAT NOISE by Dominic Finocchiaro
TWO PIGEONS EXACTLY THE SAME by Emily Feldman
THE WHITE CASTLE by Anderson John Heinz

Blind

Gloria Calderon Kellett

BLIND was produced as part of the Samuel French Off Off Broadway Short Play Festival at the East 13th Street Theatre in New York City on August 9, 2015. The performance was directed by Gloria Calderon Kellett. The cast was as follows:

WOMAN . . . . Gloria Calderon Kellett
MAN . . . . Todd Grinnell

CHARACTERS

WOMAN
MAN

(A **WOMAN** *sits typing on a laptop and drinking coffee. A* **MAN**, *standing nearby, holding a coffee, stares at her. She stares back. There is a tense-ish moment where she is wondering what the hell is going on. Then…*)

WOMAN. What?

MAN. Are you Erin?

WOMAN. No.

MAN. Oh. Okay, sorry.

> (*The* **MAN** *seems confused. He then looks around for somewhere to sit. But everything is occupied. He stands drinking his coffee and begins scrolling through his phone.*)

WOMAN. Who's Erin?

MAN. Huh? Oh, a girl.

WOMAN. Well, yeah, I would hope so since you thought I was she. If Erin ends up being a dude, I'll be pretty pissed. I mean…is she a job interview, a date? She's a date, isn't she? I can smell your cologne from here.

MAN. You can't wear cologne to a job interview?

WOMAN. No. Really any applied scent is iffy even on a date. What if she has allergies? Or hates your cologne? Really for both you should just bathe.

MAN. Good tip.

WOMAN. Lucky for you, you smell good. So…OkCupid? eHarmony? Tinder?

MAN. No. No.

> (*giving in*)

Set up.

WOMAN. Blind date. Really? People still do that?

MAN. Yeah. My buddy from work set it up.

WOMAN. Male or female. This buddy?

MAN. Male.

WOMAN. And how does he know…I'm sorry, I already forgot her name.

MAN. Erin.

WOMAN. Erin.

MAN. He went to college with her.

WOMAN. Did they ever date?

MAN. No.

WOMAN. Why not?

MAN. I don't know.

WOMAN. Is she good looking?

MAN. I think so.

WOMAN. You think so? Do you not know what she looks like?

MAN. I don't actually.

WOMAN. You didn't ask for a picture?

MAN. No.

WOMAN. Why the hell not?

MAN. Well, if you must know.

WOMAN. Well, now I'm invested.

MAN. I'm in a place in my life where I just want to meet someone great. I don't want it to be about how she looks. I thought if I saw a picture then I'd just start to make judgements or project things. I wanted this to be truly blind.

WOMAN. You, sir, are brave.

MAN. She was supposed to be wearing jeans, and a white T-shirt. And my buddy said she was a brunette with big —

(He stops. A mini beat.)

WOMAN. Boobs?

MAN. Yeah.

WOMAN. I'll take it. But that's not a very original outfit. And a T-shirt on a first date? For shame. Those first dates one should slut it up. Show the goods. I can't believe you didn't ask for a picture. You didn't Facebook her, or do a Google image search? There are ways. You know her last name? I can do it right now.

MAN. I trust my buddy. He said she's cute.

WOMAN. If she's so cute then why does she need to be set up?

MAN. I don't know. I guess she just got out of a long term relationship or something so…she's looking to get back out there. Why am I telling you this?

WOMAN. Has she seen a picture of you?

MAN. I don't think so.

WOMAN. What's your Facebook profile pic?

MAN. It's my dog.

WOMAN. Awwww. But you do know that people who put pics of their pets or their kids as their profile pic are fat. It's true. That's a thing.

MAN. That's not a thing.

WOMAN. Yeah, it is. If she Facebooked you she's gonna think you're a fatty.

MAN. That's not a thing. No. My sister's profile is of her kid — oh yeah. She didn't Facebook me.

WOMAN. Okay. But if she did. What did you tell your friend to tell her about you.

MAN. I didn't tell him to tell her anything.

WOMAN. You should have told him exactly what to tell her. What do you think he said?

MAN. I don't know. That I'm a good guy, I guess.

WOMAN. Are you?

MAN. Yes.

(beat)

WOMAN. Are you?

MAN. Yes!

WOMAN. Do you think your friend told her you were cute?

MAN. I don't know. Am I cute?

(She smiles. She likes him.)

WOMAN. Do you want to sit at my table?

MAN. I shouldn't. She'll be here any minute.

WOMAN. I'm not asking you to fuck me on it. I'm asking you to sit at it while you wait. There's nowhere else for you to sit and we're having a conversation. This is happening…so…

MAN. I guess I could sit.

(He does.)

WOMAN. I think she'll be plenty surprised. By your looks. For the record.

MAN. Yeah?

WOMAN. Yeah. You're cute. You know you're cute.

MAN. Thank you. So are you.

WOMAN. Whoa. Are you flirting with me?

MAN. No!

(then)

Maybe. Sorry.

WOMAN. No this is good. Flirt. Practice.

MAN. This is my first blind date, ok? I just didn't want you to think I do these often.

WOMAN. I wasn't judging you.

MAN. I don't normally rely on friends to set me up but, frankly, it's hard to meet someone when you're working as much as I do. And I'm not into the whole internet thing. No offense if you are. I just can't scroll through photos of girls like they're food items on a Denny's menu. And I'm looking to settle down.

WOMAN. I didn't realize you had a huge vagina. C'mon. Guys tend not to be the ones who want to settle down. Did something happen recently? Did someone die?

MAN. Sort of. My last single guy friend got married.

WOMAN. That'll do it.

MAN. Yeah, he said something that really clicked with me. I think I was getting tripped up on this whole idea of "the one" and having to be with the same person forever. It's heavy. But what he said was really interesting.

He was like… "Listen man, if you're working, you're probably only spending, like, an hour or so a day with your spouse." Plus, I play poker with my buddies, I'm on a weekend softball team, I got friends and family to see. That breaks down to maybe ten hours or so on the weekend. So, now you're looking at spending less than twenty hours a week with them. And after kids even less. So, can I find someone to be with for less than twenty hours a week? Why, yes, I think I can. Let's do this.

WOMAN. That is terrible. That is the worst thing I've ever heard.

MAN. Is it?

WOMAN. Yes.

MAN. Is it?

WOMAN. YES!

MAN. AIDS. Starving children. A dog with a broken leg.

WOMAN. Okay. Take it easy.

MAN. I'm telling you we're walking around going about life all wrong. I've thought about this long and hard and I've realized what I really want. You ready for this? Buckle up. I want "average."

WOMAN. No.

MAN. See, you're thinking of it as a bad thing but it's not. I think the problem with people is that they want too much. We've been taught to expect perfect. To expect happiness. No wonder everyone I know is on anti-depressants. It's too hard. Happiness. I just want to be content. Think about how much more attainable and sustainable that sounds. A good cup of coffee can make me content. Right now in this moment I am content. You feel that? Well I do. I spent too much of my life trying to be the best. Always got A's but what does that get you? I couldn't tell you. The people I know with the most money and the hottest girlfriends aren't the happiest. They just look the best on Christmas cards. It's all Instagram filters. It's curating the best photoshopped and posed moments of your life and putting them out there as fact. It's not real.

WOMAN. Just yesterday a friend who I know is going through a rough patch in her marriage posted pictures of an anniversary dinner her husband made for her. Pictures of each beautiful course. The bed with rose petals. Her manicured feet sticking out of a bubble bath. And I couldn't help but think of her husband. He's obviously trying like hell to save their marriage. And he must be standing there like — why are you just taking pictures and staring at your phone to see if people like this. How about you just like it. And for that matter how about you just like me. Like me! We spend more time liking things on electronics than we do liking things in real life.

MAN. Exactly! That's what I'm talking about. That's why when my last single buddy got married I realized…what am I doing? Look at this guy. Look how content he is. Is his wife Giselle? No. But she's super cool and teaches yoga. He's moving out of the city. He's buying a mid-sized house. He traded in his leased Jag for a Honda and he's the most content I've ever seen him. So, yeah, that's why I said "yes" to this blind date. Because I'm not looking for perfect anymore.

WOMAN. How is this not just a rationalization for settling?

MAN. Good question. I've thought about that, too. It's actually the opposite. It's about asking yourself honestly what you want and what you need. I'm getting real with what I really want. I'm breaking it down. You know what I want when I get home? Someone who is happy to see me. What do you want when you get home? Just…be honest? First thing that comes to your—

WOMAN. A hug.

MAN. Nice. How hard is a hug? Answer? Not that hard. You know what else I want? Someone who has interesting things to say and someone whose day I actually want to hear about. Like how many people's day do you want to hear about?

WOMAN. Like, two, maybe.

MAN. If that, right? And I'll be so sweet to her, and I'll be grateful when she remembers to buy me my favorite beer, we'll live in our little Pottery Barn house, work our 9-5 jobs we're ambivalent about, we'll come home, order some takeout, watch a little Netflix, have some pretty good sex and go to sleep. That sounds like a freaking dream come true to me. That would make me so content. And I think I could make someone, maybe Erin, content, too.

WOMAN. You make mediocrity sound romantic.

MAN. I think it is. I think when you look back on what matters it's the little moments of nothing that mean everything. And I think people would kill for a life like that. I mean, come on, doesn't that sound kinda great?

WOMAN. Yeah.

(A beat. There is something between them. MAN *breaks the moment and looks at his watch.)*

MAN. Well, I think I've been stood up. I think I'm just gonna go. Listen if you see someone with dark hair, a white shirt, and big boobs will you tell her I left. It was really nice talking to you—

(He stands.)

WOMAN. Yeah. It was.

*(*MAN *begins to walk away.)*

Wait. I have to tell you something.

*(*MAN *turns.)*

MAN. Yeah, I have to tell you something, too.

WOMAN. What?

MAN. I lied. Earlier.

WOMAN. You did?

MAN. Yeah. I saw a picture

(She is stunned.)

WOMAN. You did.

MAN. Yeah. Hi Erin.

(There is another beat.)

WOMAN. So, you knew this whole time?

MAN. Yup.

WOMAN. Why didn't you say anything?

MAN. Why didn't I say anything? Why didn't you say anything?

WOMAN. I don't know. It's too much pressure. A blind date. I was already talking myself out of it and then you walk in and you look nothing like your softball team championship photo. Not sure when that was taken but it does not do you justice. Anyway that's the picture that came up of you when I Google imaged you. And I did Facebook you and saw your adorable golden retriever and I thought you might be a little chubs and that took some of the pressure off. And then you walk in and you look like you just stepped out of a J. Crew ad. Like, your hair alone is perfection. Do you just wake up and it does that? 'Cause, wow? And I just — nothing about me is as perfect as your hair. And the thought of you walking over and realizing that I was me. And the certain wave of disappointment that would wash over your face — well, I couldn't do it. I'm sorry that I subjected you to a bag of crazy. 'Cause you seem like a very nice J. Crew ad. And uh, you know what? Please let me buy your coffee. 'Cause I think you enjoyed that and at least this wasn't a total waste 'cause…you know, free coffee.

(She pulls out a wallet and tears it apart searching for cash. All she has is a twenty.)

Do you have change for a twen — you know what? Just take the twenty.

(She lays the twenty dollar bill on the table and covers her face in shame. A beat. Neither move.)

Please take the twenty. God, please take the twenty.

(He doesn't. She looks and it's still there. She turns to look at him. He stares at her, charmed.)

What?

MAN. Are you Erin?

(She is moved by this second chance.)

WOMAN. Yes. I'm Erin.

MAN. It's nice to meet you, Erin.

WOMAN. It's nice to meet you, too.

*(**MAN** smiles and sits down as we…)*

(fade to black)

Evelyn Shaffer and the Chance of a Lifetime

Greg Edwards & Andy Roninson

EVELYN SHAFFER AND THE CHANCE OF A LIFETIME was originally produced as a podcast by Take a Ten Musicals on September 1, 2014. The cast was as follows:

EVELYN SHAFFER	Ariana Shore
TIM BECK	Ryan Andes
RECEPTIONIST	Michael Burgo
ELEVATOR	Jennifer Piacenti

EVELYN SHAFFER AND THE CHANCE OF A LIFETIME was subsequently produced as part of the Samuel French Off Off Broadway Short Play Festival at the East 13th Street Theatre in New York City on August 9, 2015. The performance was directed by Jess Chayes. The cast was as follows:

EVELYN SHAFFER	Victoria Huston-Elem
TIM BECK	Ben Beckleys
RECEPTIONIST	Rob Hille

CHARACTERS

EVELYN SHAFFER – an indie game designer
TIM BECK – the head of Moonbeam Studios
RECEPTIONIST – a disgruntled employee

SETTING

Moonbeam Studios, a wildly successful video game developer. Present day.

SONGS

"Evelyn Shaffer and the Chance of a Lifetime"......Evelyn, Receptionist
"On the Other Side of the Screen" .... Evelyn
"Game On"... Evelyn

MUSIC

For use of the Keyboard Orchestration and Performance Instrumental Tracks, licensees should visit evelynmusical.com.

(**EVELYN** *stands outside an office building, the headquarters of Moonbeam Studios.*)

EVELYN.
OKAY, EVELYN. KEEP IT IN CHECK.
YOUR BRAIN'S ON ALERT.
YOUR FEET ARE INERT.
BE SMART AND ASSERTIVE, AND YOU'RE SURE TO ACE THIS INTERVIEW.

OKAY, EVELYN. YOU'RE MEETING TIM BECK.
HE'S JUST A GAME DESIGNER,
SO THINK OF HIM AS MINOR.
HE'S ONLY THE DEFINER OF THE FIELD YOU PURSUE.

ONE INTERVIEW, AND YOU COULD GO FROM INDIE TO THE PROS.
IT'S LIKE YOU'RE IN A GAME, AND HERE'S THE TITLE
I PROPOSE:

"EVELYN SHAFFER
AND THE CHANCE OF A LIFETIME."
SHE THOUGHT SHE WAS A ZERO
WHO COULD NEVER MAKE THE CUT.
NOW, EVELYN SHAFFER
HAS THE CHANCE OF A LIFETIME,
AND SOON YOU'LL SEE OUR HERO
KICKING BUTT.

(*She enters the building. A* **RECEPTIONIST** *greets her in a monotone.*)

RECEPTIONIST. Welcome to Moonbeam Studios. How may I help you?
EVELYN. Hi, I have an appointment with Mr. Beck.
RECEPTIONIST. Evelyn Shaffer?
EVELYN. Present!

RECEPTIONIST. Follow me. And please keep your voice down; the designers are at work.

(The RECEPTIONIST leads EVELYN through the office.)

EVELYN. *(Quietly)*
OKAY, EVELYN. YOU'RE REALLY INSIDE,
AND HERE ON THIS FLOOR,
MERE DECADES BEFORE,
THEY WROTE ALL THE STORIES THAT GOT YOU THROUGH THE LONELY YEARS.

RECEPTIONIST. You okay?

EVELYN. Sure am!

I THINK I JUST DIED.
I MADE IT TO MY MECCA
A BLOCK ABOVE TRIBECA.
THEIR OFFICE IS SO DECADENT. THE CUBICLES ARE SPHERES!

FOR YEARS, I ONLY DREAMED IT. NOW, I'M *IN* THEIR STUDIO.
AND MAYBE IF I'M GOOD ENOUGH, I'LL NEVER HAVE TO GO.

CAUSE EVELYN SHAFFER
HAS THE CHANCE OF A LIFETIME.
IMAGINE MY TOMORROW
IF I MAKE IT THROUGH TODAY
WHEN EVELYN SHAFFER
MAYBE ONCE IN HER LIFETIME
CAN FINALLY MAKE THE SORROW
FADE AWAY.

*(They reach an **ELEVATOR**. Its doors open. Ding.)*

RECEPTIONIST. Step inside the elevator, please. Mr. Beck's office is on the thirtieth floor.

SEXY ELEVATOR. *(Voiceover)* "Doors closing."

(A beat, then:)

RECEPTIONIST. It's a very slow elevator.

EVELYN.
WHEN YOU'RE A CHILD,

THERE ARE GAMES YOU PLAY
AND STORIES YOU HEAR
THAT STICK TO YOU,
THAT BEND YOU,
THAT CHANGE THE WAY YOU SEE.
SO WHAT COULD BE MORE FINE
THAN TO DREAM AND THEN DESIGN
A GAME THAT CAN CHANGE WHO A PERSON WILL BE,
THAT GIVES HER THE HOPE THAT MOONBEAM GAVE ME?

    (ding)

SEXY ELEVATOR. *(Voiceover)* "Thirtieth floor."

RECEPTIONIST. Mr. Beck is the last door on the right. Please knock before entering, and have a euphoric day.

    (**EVELYN** *walks down the hall.*)

EVELYN.
IT'S EVELYN SHAFFER
AND THE CHANCE OF A LIFETIME,
WHERE PRESENT, PAST, AND FUTURE
UNMISTAKABLY ALIGN,
CAUSE EVELYN SHAFFER
IS SO CLOSE TO HER LIFETIME DREAM!
THOUGH I'D NEVER SUGGEST ANY
WORKINGS OF DESTINY,
THIS MOMENT HAS TO BE A SIGN
THAT THE CHANCE OF A LIFETIME—

    (*She knocks on the door to* **TIM BECK**'s *office.*)

WILL BE MINE!

    (*Inside the office,* **TIM BECK** *gets up to greet her.*)

TIM BECK. Evelyn Shaffer, come in, come in. You find the place okay?

EVELYN. Oh, I've walked by the Moonbeam Tower for years. But I never thought I'd get to come inside and interview with you.

TIM BECK. Interview, who said anything about an interview?

EVELYN. Well, I assumed—

TIM BECK. Please, this is much friendlier than that. Now, last week, I stumbled across your game.

EVELYN. *Penelope Pontraine and the City of Mystery?*

TIM BECK. Loved Penelope, loved her. Plucky young heroine, solving puzzles and unravelling mysteries using nothing but her wits. You've created an amazing character. How old is she? Nineteen?

EVELYN. Twelve.

TIM BECK. Right. You come so close to the Moonbeam standard. You do so much with so little. And with us, you could do so much more. So I want to hire you to develop *Penelope* here at Moonbeam.

EVELYN. What, I'm, I…don't know what to say…

TIM BECK. "Yes" is a great start. We've already got some of Moonbeam's top designers taking a crack at *Penelope*, and they're more than happy to collaborate with you! Just look at their concept art.

(He hands her a stack of papers.)

EVELYN. Oh, gosh…wow.

TIM BECK. Rocking, no?

EVELYN. Penelope…she has, um…

(Her hands drift toward her chest.)

TIM BECK. Our research has found that players connect to characters who are physically *mature*.

EVELYN. And is that a gun?

TIM BECK. If she doesn't have a gun, how is she going to kill Nazis?

EVELYN. Well, actually, there isn't really killing in—
Nazis?

TIM BECK. Look, Evelyn, my old adventure games, like *The Curse of the Pirate King*…

EVELYN. I loved that game.

TIM BECK. You and I are the only ones who did. It didn't even move five thousand units. Since then, Moonbeam has found broader appeal with our action franchises, like *Maxx Warfare* and *I Have No Hands But I Must Stab.*

EVELYN. But Penelope—

TIM BECK. Evelyn, how long have you been gaming?

EVELYN. Since I was a little girl.

TIM BECK. Then I want you to think about the smiles on the faces of millions of little girls as they clutch their own copy of *Penelope Pontraine*. And below Penelope's name, it'll have yours and mine, right next to each other. "By Evelyn Shaffer and Tim Beck."

EVELYN. On the same box?

TIM BECK. Now, isn't that worth a little collaboration?

(then)

Here, take a moment to think it over. I'll go check on the paperwork.

(He exits. **EVELYN** *stares at the concept art.)*

EVELYN.
AS A KID, WHEN I GOT HOME FROM SCHOOL,
I'D RUN TO THE TV
AND FIRE UP OUR 8-BIT N.E.S.
IN THE HOURS THAT I PLAYED,
I FELT THE REAL WORLD FADE.
IN RETROSPECT, IT'S SILLY,
I GUESS.

BUT ON THE OTHER SIDE OF THE SCREEN,
I HAD A PURPOSE.
AS I JUMPED ACROSS EACH RAVINE,
I HAD A GOAL.
NEVER LOST,
NEVER SMALL,
NEVER LIKE ME AT ALL,
ON THE OTHER SIDE OF THE SCREEN,
I WAS WHOLE.

SURE, I HAD A LIFE BEYOND THE GAMES,
AND OFTEN IT WAS NICE.
SOME LONELINESS, I GUESS. I DIDN'T MIND.

I HAD FRIENDS, AT LEAST A FEW,
AT TIMES, A FATHER TOO,
BUT STILL I WANTED SOMETHING MORE…
DESIGNED.

AND ON THE OTHER SIDE OF THE SCREEN,
MY WORLD WAS STEADY,
A DOMAIN OF RULES AND ROUTINE
WHERE I FIT IN.
I COULD PLAN,
PERSEVERE.
THE INSTRUCTIONS WERE CLEAR.
ON THE OTHER SIDE OF THE SCREEN,
I COULD WIN.

FOR IF TIME RAN OUT
OR I FELL TOO FAR,
I COULD ALWAYS START ANEW.
FOR I WAS MORE THAN ME,
I WAS MY AVATAR.
OH, HOW I LONGED TO CROSS INTO—

THE OTHER SIDE OF THE SCREEN
WHERE I WAS BETTER,
WHERE I'D HURTLE TOWARD THE UNSEEN,
EAGER TO ROAM.
UNABASHED,
UNAFRAID,
OH, MEMORIES I MADE.
ON THE OTHER SIDE OF THE SCREEN,
I HAD AN ESCAPE.

No.

ON THE OTHER SIDE OF THE SCREEN,
I HAD A HOME.

*(**TIM BECK** returns.)*

TIM BECK. Good news. If you sign with us today, we can have *Penelope* on sale in time for the holidays.

EVELYN. I'm sorry, I can't do it.

TIM BECK. Uh…excuse me?

EVELYN. I can't betray Penelope. She would never do it to me.

TIM BECK. Of course she wouldn't. She's a fictional character. And possibly a plush doll.

EVELYN. I'm sorry, but I can't.

TIM BECK. Listen, Evelyn, maybe you don't understand how this business works. We make games, we sell games. If we don't sell millions of copies, how do we keep the studio open?

EVELYN. And if you make *Penelope Pontraine and the Nazi Zombies…*

TIM BECK. Good title.

EVELYN. …then who cares if the studio's open or shut?

(A beat, then:)

TIM BECK. I think we're done here. In this business, you get one chance. *That* was yours.

(She walks to the door.)

EVELYN. You were talented once. You know that.

TIM BECK. And once, I thought you were smart.

*(**EVELYN** closes the door behind her.)*

EVELYN.
EVERY STORY NEEDS A HERO
TO SLAY THE DRAGON, SCALE THE WALL,
AND HERE I THOUGHT I HAD ONE,
BUT SOMETIMES HEROES FALL.
WELL, I'M NO PRINCESS IN A TOWER
PINING NIGHT AND DAY.
THE HERO SAID GAME OVER,
BUT THAT'S OKAY
CAUSE ME I SAY—

GAME ON,
BRING THE DANGER AND THE GLORY.
GAME ON,
BRING ME STRAIGHT INTO THE SCRUM,

AND I KNOW
I'LL BECOME
THE NEW HERO OF MY STORY.
SEE, MY SWORD IS DRAWN.
GAME ON.

THOUGH THE ROAD IS FULL OF MONSTERS,
ALL RAZOR-FANGED AND BEADY-EYED,
I KNOW THEY CAN'T BE HALF AS BAD
AS THOSE I'VE HAD INSIDE,
SO I'LL BLAZE FORWARD ON MY QUEST
THROUGH FOREST BLACK AS NIGHT,
AND SHOULD THE HORDE ATTACK ME—
WELL, THAT'S ALRIGHT
CAUSE I CAN FIGHT.

GAME ON,
BRING THE DANGER AND THE GLORY.
GAME ON,
BRING ADVENTURE FRAUGHT WITH CHANCE,
AND I SWEAR
I'LL ADVANCE
TO NEW LEVELS OF MY STORY
TIL THE FEAR IS GONE—

THE FEAR THAT, LIKE SO MANY PLAYERS, I CANNOT PREVAIL,
THAT NO MATTER WHAT I DO, I TOO MAY FALL OR FLEE OR FAIL.
IT'S TRUE NOT EVERYONE SURVIVES
THE PERILS OF THE PLOT,
BUT WHO NEEDS EXTRA LIVES?
I LOVE THE LIFE I GOT,
SO READY OR NOT—

>   *(Headlines appear behind **EVELYN**: "Penelope Sells a Million Copies!," "Shaffer Starts Own Studio!," "Shaffer Awarded Nobel Prize in Video Gameology!")*

GAME ON,
NOW I FIND MY WAY TO GLORY.
GAME ON,

NOW I JOURNEY TOWARD THE SUN,
FOR MY TALE
HAS BEGUN,
I'M THE TELLER OF MY STORY,
AND THE FEAR IS GONE.
GAME ON!

Narrators

Simon Henriques

NARRATORS was first produced at Production Workshop's 3 Chairs, 2 Cubes festival in Providence, RI. It opened October 24, 2014. It was directed by Naiyah Ambros. Thecast was as follows:

BILL.	Stella Mensah
WALTER.	Yuval Yossefy
STEPHEN	Richie Whitehead
FRANK.	Simon Henriques

NARRATORS was subsequently produced as part of the Samuel French Off Off Broadway Short Play Festival at the East 13th Street Theatre in New York City on August 9, 2015. The performance was directed by Skylar Fox. The cast was as follows:

BILL.	Will Ruehle
WALTER.	Sam Alper
STEPHEN	Harrison Chad
FRANK.	Simon Henriques

CHARACTERS

BILL – a narrator
WALTER – a narrator
STEPHEN – a stagehand
FRANK – a narrator

SETTING

This theater

TIME

Today

*(A stagehand, **STEPHEN**, busily prepares the set. An armchair at one corner of the stage. Center stage, a bed. When everything is set, he nods to the booth and the lights go down.)*

*(When the lights return, **BILL** is sitting in the chair, a closed book on his lap. **WALTER** is lying in bed, asleep.)*

BILL. Let's pick up where we left off, shall we?

(He opens the book and begins to read.)

After another long, exciting day, Walter had fallen asleep. He felt safe in his bed. Relaxed, peaceful. His sleep was undisturbed, and he had many dreams. He dreamt that all the people he had ever known were figures in a wax museum, and that he was a guard in that wax museum. He dreamt that he was wearing a huge feathered headdress, staring in a mirror while rain fell for miles around him. He dreamt that he built a robot and that the robot came to life and that it pierced his heart with its laser vision, and he slowly bled to death while his metal monster clinked and clanked and clunked its way out the door to replace him. After dreaming all of these dreams, Walter woke up.

*(Throughout the following, **WALTER** carries out the actions **BILL** describes, with technical assistance from **STEPHEN**.)*

Walter stepped into the bathroom for his morning shower. As the water ran over his body, Walter mentally prepared himself for the day to come. He knew that his job would be difficult, as always, but he also knew that it would be rewarding, as always. He told himself the effort would be worth it. He tried to imagine the shower as a metaphor, cleansing him of his preoccupations and letting him enter into the day purified and refreshed. Then the hot water ran out.

Walter dried off his body as best he could. He hated the feeling of putting clothes on over wet skin. Of course, he could never get himself perfectly dry, and he had to settle for simply being mostly dry. Walter had learned long ago how to cope with minor disappointments. In fact, they seemed to make up the better portion of his days.

Then Walter ate breakfast. He had cereal because it was the cheapest, and he had it with skim milk, because it was the healthiest. Everything Walter did had a cause and an effect, and he understood this. Walter's life could be broken down into a chain, or maybe several chains. But Walter never felt that these figurative chains figuratively chained him down. On the contrary. He liked the structure. He liked knowing why he did things; he liked having an easy way to remember his past; he liked to have some idea of what was going to come in his future. After rinsing out his cereal bowl, Walter left for work.

Walter hit a traffic jam on his way to work. He did every morning. Walter could have avoided this daily traffic jam if he just took a different route, and he knew this. But Walter drove straight into the traffic jam every morning. He planned enough time for it, so he wasn't late for work. He liked the routine. He liked the time to sit and contemplate. Sitting among the row of cars, Walter thought about his fellow man. Each car, he reasoned, had at least person, and each person, he reasoned, had at least one story. So a lot of cars—which there were—meant a lot of stories. Stories Walter would never know. Walter felt bad, because he liked stories and thought they should be shared. Finally, Walter arrived at work.

> (**STEPHEN** *sets up an armchair in the corner of the stage opposite* **BILL**.)

Getting to work was the best part of Walter's day. The day was full of potential, and anything could happen. Walter liked his home, but Walter loved his job. Many people hate their jobs, but Walter loved his. Walter loved his job because he had the best job in the world:

(STEPHEN hands WALTER a book.)

WALTER. Let's pick up where we left off, shall we?

BILL. being a narrator.

(WALTER opens his book.)

Walter opened his book and began to narrate.

WALTER. Bill's book was open in his lap and he was speaking in a loud, clear voice. He was very good at his job of being a narrator. He was very good at his job because he took pride in his job. Why did he take such pride in his job? Well, that's because being a narrator is the best job in the world.

BILL. As Walter began to introduce the character whose life he was narrating, his voice rang out to the audience in a rich, honeyed baritone.

WALTER. Bill had been a narrator for many years.

BILL. Walter said.

WALTER. There were certain narrator idiosyncrasies he liked to do that didn't always make sense.

BILL. Walter said.

WALTER. For example, sometimes at the end of a line of dialogue, he would append a "so-and-so said," which often made his narration clunky and bloated.

BILL. Walter said.

WALTER. *(snarky)* Bill said.

BILL. Walter said.

WALTER. Bill said.

BILL. Walter said.

WALTER. Bill said.

BILL. Walter was very good at his job.

WALTER. Despite the occasional verbal eccentricity, Bill was very good at his job.

BILL. Walter was so good at his job that he could afford to let his mind wander a bit while he narrated. Walter thought about the sandwich he had packed for lunch that afternoon. Walter thought about the songs he had heard on the radio in the traffic jam that morning. Walter thought about the dreams he had had the night before.

WALTER. Bill described thoughts. While it may seem impossible to know another person's thoughts, it was easy for Bill. He was a third-person omniscient narrator, which meant he knew everything about the characters whose lives he narrated.

BILL. In Walter's dreams, if you'll recall, he was a guard in a wax museum filled with all the people he had ever known. In Walter's dreams, rain fell for miles around him while he stared at himself in a mirror, wearing a huge feathered headdress. In Walter's dreams, a robot he built attacked and subsequently replaced him.

WALTER. Sometimes, Bill's third-person omniscience meant he knew details about his characters that even they didn't know.

BILL. Walter kept thinking about his dreams. Much in the same way he liked to fantasize symbolic significance to his morning shower, he believed each dream he dreamt had meaningful psychological weight. In reality, he wasn't sure whether or not they really did. In reality, he wasn't sure about very much at all.

WALTER. Bill barely even realized his own power.

BILL. Walter wanted to talk about these dreams, these thoughts, these questions, but he couldn't. He was at work, and his job wasn't to talk about himself. It was to talk about other people. So he kept his ideas to himself and kept on doing what he was doing.

WALTER. Bill understood the characters whose lives he narrated. He saw through them to their core.

BILL. Still, no matter how much he talked about other people, the images from his dreams haunted him: the wax, the headdress, the rain, the robot.

WALTER. Bill talked about how the character whose life he was narrating was recollecting his dreams, and Bill thought about those dreams, too. They weren't his dreams but he felt a part of them regardless. That can happen to a narrator who becomes truly invested in a story they're telling—they can begin to feel like a character in that story, rather than someone on the outside looking in.

BILL. Walter philosophized on the nature of narration itself.

WALTER. Bill described his character's philosophizing on the nature of narration itself, and couldn't help but do the same.

BILL. Narration was a funny thing to do, Walter thought.

WALTER. It didn't seem immediately useful, Bill thought.

BILL. But he still intuitively knew it was an important job.

WALTER. After all, he reasoned, if it weren't for narrators, who would tell the world's stories?

BILL. And how could a story be heard if there was no one to tell it?

WALTER. And what good was a story if no one heard it?

> (**STEPHEN** *comes onstage and signals* **BILL**, *who marks his place in his book and gets up to stretch his legs.*)

Bill was informed that he was due for a quick break. He was given a short rest every hour in the terms of his contract, which was very reasonable. Sometimes his legs fell asleep when he sat in that armchair for such a long time, and it was good to walk around to keep his blood flowing.

> (**STEPHEN** *gives* **BILL** *a cup of coffee. He drinks it.*)

WALTER. Bill drank coffee on his breaks to keep him focused and alert. While the energy boost was considerable, coffee doesn't do much good for the voice. Bill was vaguely aware of this, but he didn't care to focus on it.

BILL. Frenetic friends frantically fuck. Frenetic friends frantically fuck. Frenetic friends frantically fuck.

WALTER. Bill ran through some tongue twisters to keep his mouth limbered up. He liked to do risqué tongue twisters, because his life was not very risqué. Saying such vulgar things was just one more perk of his job.

(Upon another signal from **STEPHEN**, **BILL** *returns to his seat.)*

Bill's break quickly ended. He was thankful they were so short; he liked the structure his work provided him. He never needed to worry about what came next when he was doing his job.

BILL. Let's pick up where we left off, shall we?

(opens the book)

After narrating a relatively calm passage which he took advantage of to work in some background detail, Walter was feeling tired. He hadn't been at work for very long, but he was ready to move on to a different story.

WALTER. Let's leave Bill for now.

BILL. And that's enough of Walter's life for today.

*(***STEPHEN*** takes the books from* **BILL** *and* **WALTER** *and gives them each a new one.)*

BILL/WALTER. Let's pick up where we left off, shall we?

(They open the books.)

BILL. Stephen was hard at work.

WALTER. He had just given two narrators new books and taken away their old ones.

BILL. Any time someone onstage needed something given to them or taken away from them, Stephen was there to help out.

WALTER. It was his job. Stephen was a stagehand.

BILL. At the moment, Stephen didn't have anything to do. The two narrators were going to be reading from their new books for a while, and they wouldn't need anything given to them or taken away from them.

WALTER. So Stephen took advantage of the downtime to let his mind wander.

BILL. Stephen thought about all the moments whose staged representations he had helped facilitate that day.

WALTER. He thought about the first scene he had set up that night, in which a character lay in bed and dreamed.

BILL. Stephen thought about that character's dreams.

WALTER. In that character's dreams, all the people he had ever known were figures in a wax museum, and that he was a guard in that wax museum.

BILL. In that character's dreams, he stared into a mirror wearing a feathered headdress, while rain fell all around him.

WALTER. In that character's dreams, a robot he built killed him and took his place in the outside world.

BILL. Stephen thought the dreams were interesting. Stephen wished his dreams were that interesting.

WALTER. Stephen wished he could find someone to love and maybe raise a parakeet with.

BILL. But what Stephen wished for, more than anything else in the world,

WALTER. was to be a narrator.

BILL. It's not hard to blame him. Being a narrator is the best job in the world.

WALTER. So it was only natural for Stephen to aspire to that loftiest of occupations.

BILL. Stephen didn't think it was very likely that he would ever move beyond being a stagehand, let alone become a narrator,

WALTER. but he still liked to fantasize about it every now and again.

> (**STEPHEN** *enters, dragging an armchair to the middle of the stage.*)

BILL. Sometimes, when he thought no one was watching, he would sit in an armchair.

WALTER. An armchair like the ones the narrators sat in.

BILL. The real narrators, the bigshots, with their books.

STEPHEN. Let's, uh…ahem. Let's pick up where we left off, shall we?

BILL. While Stephen loved to pretend, he never opened the books. Only the true narrators were allowed to do that.

WALTER. But today, Stephen decided to throw caution to the wind.

BILL. He did something very, very wrong.

WALTER. He grabbed life by the horns

BILL. and made a huge mistake.

WALTER. He opened the book.

STEPHEN. *(reading, confused)* Stephen…read out loud from the book. He quickly realized that he wasn't supposed to have seen its pages, but that didn't stop him from continuing.

WALTER. *(overlapping)* Stephen was consumed with the thrill of discovery.

STEPHEN. He flipped eagerly through the book, turning page after page, hoping for some juicy glimpse into his own future.

BILL. *(overlapping)* Stephen would soon see the problem with his actions.

STEPHEN. But no matter how far Stephen read, the book would only say that Stephen continued to read. Because if he read a page then he was reading and the page was what he did so if what he did was read then that's what the page would say. Stephen was beginning to realize he was in way over his head.

BILL. Stephen used a cliché to describe his situation, but that was to be expected from a rookie narrator.

WALTER. That's when Stephen got a new idea.

BILL. If Stephen's decision to open the book was unheard of, this next one was even more so, albeit in a different sort of way.

WALTER. Stephen closed the book.

> *(STEPHEN closes the book and puts it on the ground. After a deep breath, he addresses the audience.)*

STEPHEN. Let's pick up where we left off, shall we?

BILL. Stephen began to narrate without a book.

STEPHEN. So there were these two narrators. One was named Bill and the other was named Walter. They were both really good at their jobs. And they had a stagehand who helped them out: me.

WALTER. Stephen inserted himself into his narration. He was not working in third-person omniscience, as was the industry standard. Instead, he spoke in the first person. He was not omniscient.

STEPHEN. Bill was, like, sixty.

BILL. This meant he sometimes got things wrong.

STEPHEN. Walter was younger, but they both seemed infinitely old and wise, like they knew secrets that you couldn't even begin to understand, like they had keys for locks in doors you hadn't ever realized were there.

It came with the territory of being a professional narrator. They had the answers to so many questions. And that was probably why they loved narrating so much. In fact, that was the only time either one of them ever really seemed happy.

One day — today. Ugh. HI. HELLO. I'm Stephen. I'm a stagehand. But I want to be a narrator. I want to be a narrator because I like stories. See, stories connect people to one another. They're like a bridge between… this side of a river and that side of a river. The sides of the river are people. But I'm not sure if that's true anymore, because Bill and Walter talk about each other a *lot* and they've still never talked *to* each other.

(BILL and WALTER are caught off guard by this. They turn to face one another.)

STEPHEN. Sorry. I shouldn't have—That was wrong.
BILL. No.
WALTER. It's all right.
STEPHEN. Oh. Um.

(An uncomfortable pause. BILL, WALTER, and STEPHEN look at each other.)

(A voice comes on over the sound system.)

FRANK. Bill and Walter and Stephen had nothing more to say.

(BILL, WALTER, and STEPHEN continue looking at one another, apparently unaware of this voice.)

This was uncommon. It was uncomfortable. It was scary: what happened when the narrators stopped telling their stories? Would the world come screeching to a halt?

(The trio turns out to look at the audience.)

Probably not. And the realization of this made Bill and Walter and Stephen feel like it was time to go home, take a couple Tums, and lie down for a while.

(BILL, WALTER, and STEPHEN produce bottles of Tums. They each take two. It doesn't help.)

The Tums didn't help, of course, because this was a problem of the mind or of the heart or of the soul, but not of the stomach. Still, taking Tums was a nice concrete step they could take, and that felt helpful in itself.

(BILL, WALTER, and STEPHEN prepare to go to sleep on the floor of the theater.)

That night, Bill lay awake in bed and thought about his father, who had also been a narrator, and how he was upholding years of tradition. Walter lay awake in bed and thought about sitting in traffic, and how maybe it was time to rethink which roads he took. Stephen lay awake in bed and thought about open books and closed books and hearts in cages being nibbled at by birds.

All three of them stared up at white blank ceilings that stretched out for miles, or years, full of empty. The next day would bring a new chapter. Neither Bill nor Walter nor Stephen knew what that day-chapter would hold. More stories, probably. More questions without answers, certainly. But for now, it was time for them all to close their eyes and hope the dreams were pleasant.

> (**BILL**, **WALTER**, and **STEPHEN** *close their eyes and go to sleep. It feels like the play should end, but it doesn't. The lights don't go down.*)

I'm sorry. I don't really know if that —

Here's a recipe for deviled eggs, so you at least feel like you're coming away with *some*thing from all this. Uh, ingredients. Seven large eggs, hard-boiled and peeled. A quarter cup of mayonnaise. One and a half tablespoons of sweet pickle relish. One teaspoon of mustard. Salt and pepper, to taste. Paprika, sweet gherkin pickles, sliced, pimentos, all for garnish.

Okay, here's what you're gonna wanna do with all that. Halve the eggs lengthwise. Remove yolks and place in a small bowl. Mash yolks with a fork and stir in mayonnaise, pickle relish, mustard, and salt and pepper. Fill egg whites evenly with yolk mixture. Garnish with paprika, pickles, and pimentos. Store covered in refrigerator.

And now you know how to make deviled eggs.

Seabird is in a Happy Place

James Gordon King

SEABIRD IS IN A HAPPY PLACE was first produced as part of Babelle Theatre's RIVULETS: THREE SHORT PLAYS ABOUT A FLOOD at the Lone Pine Studio in Vancouver in July of 2015. It was directed and dramaturged by Marie Farsi. The scenic designer was Carolyn Rapanos, lighting designer was Andrew Pye, and the composer/sound designer was Paul Paroczai. The production stage manager was Scarlett Larry. The cast was as follows:

SEABIRD . . . . Emilie Leclerc

SEABIRD IS IN A HAPPY PLACE was subsequently produced as part of the Samuel French Off Off Broadway Short Play Festival at the East 13th Street Theatre in New York City on August 9, 2015 with the same director and cast.

CHARACTERS

SEABIRD – a woman in her twenties. Seabird lives in her body more than she does her head. Her pace is always energetic, sometimes unconsidered and sometimes uncontrolled.

SETTING

A city in North America.

TIME

The future.

AUTHOR'S NOTES

The following should be told to the audience as though it were testimony. Rain doesn't need to be consistent throughout the entire play, but suggestions have been made as to the points where it should start, slow down, pick-up, etc.

(**SEABIRD** *is onstage, wearing a red track suit.*)

SEABIRD. I fucked up.
   I don't know why I did it.
   I knew I was being irresponsible.
   I knew I was being selfish.
   But you should've seen her:
   tucked in the doorway of Anne's bar,
   smoking a cigarette.
   Yo, she looked so serious.
   It was like this cigarette was the most important cigarette anyone had ever fucking smoked,
   you know what I mean?
   I wanted to destroy her.
   I thought about hurricane winds,
   running up and smashing through an old house, that rush of coming apart, you know?
   I knew that.
   Her face…
   the way she'd hold her cigarette…
   like she thought no one was looking.
   She'd smoke like this…and…
   I thought it was perfect…
   those dry chapped lips…
   So I step over and I'm like
   "Yo, here's some lip balm"
   and she looks at me like
   "Who the fuck are you?" and
   "Where the fuck did you get lip balm?"
   and I produce it…
   pull out my cylinder…
   apply it to my lips…

and her eyes go in real close.
Her face comes down, and I'm like:
"There."
She can't be more than twenty five years old,
but up until this point she looks forty or fifty.
She takes the lip balm, doesn't say shit, applies it to her lips,
real slow, eyeing me up…
She tells me her name is Hannah.
I tell her my name is Seabird and that Hannah is way too beautiful a woman to be scrunching her face up so seriously — which I know is something that jackasses say all the time, but I think she sees with me that I really mean it.
I have her laughing, I smoke one of her cigarettes.
I don't want to waste any time so I come in right away:
"You and me: I know what makes you work. Let's go."
She looks at me, like, "Damn, where did you come from?" and I'm like,
"You're holding onto shit, I can see it. I can see that you're scared and that maybe you don't trust yourself, but let's go.
Trust me."
Now I have never spoken this way before. Am I making an impression?
We go back inside Anne's, have a beer, and then head back to her place to fuck.

> *(light shift)*
>
> *(beat)*

I get it.
You didn't ask to be here.
There was nobody holding your hand and checking whether or not this is what you wanted or whether or not this time period worked.

Of course you dig your heels, because you don't want to be pushed.
You only want to do things when you're ready.
Well, opportunity doesn't arrive one day, like,
"is this eight o' clock? Is this what we agreed upon?"
Opportunity shows up, like, "I'm fuckin' here, right?!"

    (beat)

When we're done she asks if she can see me again, and maybe this was where I fucked up...
Maybe I should've just said
"Sugar, you probably won't ever see me again,"
but instead I give her the name of this bar.
I don't know why, but I tell her that I might be there later having a drink.
And I'm really fucking stupid,
but I also really fucking like her and it looks like the rain will hold up until the morning
at least...

    (beat)

    (sound of rain falling)

See, I knew I was going to die soon,
but even if I didn't know that,
I could still have died at any fucking moment.
How are any of your promises different from mine?
You could be on a bus,
on your way to work one day,
admiring a pretty girl
arranging flowers outside a shop,
when suddenly —

    (light shift...)

You're dead.

    (beat)

Next you're in some underworld:

a windowless room, on one side of a desk
apologizing for everything you've ever done,
for every crumb you've stolen or
every bad word that you've ever said,
and gaping there across from you is this man,
like, this ordinary slouch, going
"Ms. I'm sorry you're going to die, but there's nothing I can do."
But, come on, there must be something he can do! So you press him, because "Listen, man.
Life is shitty, but it's not that shitty, you know?"
and he's like, "...Do you want me to go and see with one of my colleagues?"
and you're like,
"Yes! Please! Go and meet with your colleagues,
go meet with the devil if he fuckin' exists!"
So he goes...
And he walks back in after god knows how long,
and he brings you down this hallway into this room filled with smoke,
and then he brings you to the desk of this big unhappy looking man and introduces him, like,
"This guy's name is Rain."
And Rain hardly looks up.
Already he's slamming through drawers and shoving papers at you,
asking you to sign this and sign this...
and you're like "What the fuck am I signing?" and he says
"A conditional resurrection" and you're like
"What are the conditions?" and he says
"You come back when I come back"
and you don't really know what he means...
You're thinking to yourself, like,
"is this a negotiation? Should I have a lawyer present?"

But then there's this other voice in your head, like your mother, saying
"Seabird, don't be a fucking idiot. Sign the papers."
So you do.

> *(light shift)*

> *(beat)*

Then you're outside.
You're on this beach where Rain is saddling up horses and
you don't fuckin' know how to ride a horse, but he just pops you up on one, like,
there you go sweetie, like
it isn't even a fuckin' problem, and then you take off.
Like…
Up.

> *(beat)*

Listen, I know it sounds like a kid's book but I don't know how else to put it.
You and that horse are weightless and it feels like weeping, like
deep chested, full out, crazy ass weeping, not sad, but, like, happy, like,
you've never been so happy in your entire life.
You look down and your body is gone,
you don't know where it is,
but below you there's ocean, which,
from up here, looks the same as staring up at the sky from down there,
and that wind is blowing through you — *man*,
that wind is blowing through you like it has never done anything else and
what comes to you next is this idea:
how you don't have to go back,
you don't have to do anything,

but for some reason…
yes…

    (Beat.)

You start to descend.
You see the clouds forming up ahead, and the city below them,
you feel your body returning and falling with the rain and it's
only a minute later that you see her…
Hannah.

    (Long Beat.)

You get it, right?
I come back from the dead and the first thing I do is fuck this girl's brains out…?
It's fucked up!
But you see, I didn't take the time to analyze.
I was coming in fast, like,
head down.
There was nobody yelling at me like that voice in the office.
I mean… It felt good.
Right?

    (Beat.)

    (Light Shift.)

Obviously I should've gone to see my family.
I should've gone to see my family and all my friends and I should've said to them
"Thank you" or "Guys, it's been great. I'll miss you." or some shit like that.
But
— and this is fucked up—
I didn't feel like I had to!
I had *died*
and all that old me and all those memories,
all those fucked up fights and all that bullshit—

it was finished.
I mean, it was still being played, but I had left it,
I was out.
So I go for a walk.
Yeah. In the fucking rain.
I go out and I take my time, like,
I never have once stopped to look at this city:
big fuckin' city with its towers of glass, steel.
Monuments, tombstones for dead white men,
money, unimaginable amounts of money.
On the ground, men and women are rotting under umbrellas while directly up above
I see horses charging through the sky,
spitting and kicking up clouds!

    (Beat.)

I walk and I walk and
eventually I end up at this corner where I shouldn't be, where the water isn't running into the sewer like it should.
I see this familiar looking flower shop.
All over the sidewalk there's broken glass and steel
and in the middle of the street is the steaming skeleton of a bus
— You can still see some of the seats—
the roof peeled off, the bottom blown out.
Some black body bags are lined up getting rained on while
these soldiers in white jumpsuits are poking through everything with, like, ski-poles…?
People walking by in every direction.
I have to check myself because even I kind of feel nothing.
But I should feel something, right?
But I don't. Somehow it all belongs.
Like, this guy with the ski-pole is picking it all apart, but what if it doesn't need to be separated?

A bus full of people were randomly killed today, like,
the fact it's also raining
— Maybe neither could have been prevented!
People are always like,
this would be a perfect day if it weren't for…whatever, but
fuck that!
Who are we to say what's perfect?
Who are we to say what's tragic?
What's wrong?
What if this isn't *wrong?*
What if it just fucking *is?*
And I realize this all sounds crazy as hell, but it's *flooding me*, and…
what I feel is that
this is what I need to tell my family…
and sooner rather than later,
because already I can imagine that military steward walking up the steps of my building, that sympathetic look on his face,
hands folded out in front of his crotch…
So I start back to my neighbourhood,
soaking wet, insane,
I go back to this spot right behind the elementary school.
It's this spot low from the road
where my sister goes to smoke before she picks up her kid.
I write there in big red letters
— in *my* letters—
"Seabird is in a Happy Place"
And I think that's pretty fuckin' good for bye.

    (thunderclap)

    (light shift)

I go to this bar in question.
I make friends with a room full of strangers.
I hand all the money I have to the owner and he cracks open a couple big bottles on top the bar.
I guess everybody figures I'm about to get murdered or busted,
because I keep getting handshakes,
claps on the back, *long solemn looks.*
"Listen, I want everyone to enjoy themselves!
Tomorrow may never come so no sad faces!"
A couple guys — young guys — let out a cheer.
Then a couple more from the bar.
Suddenly I have this whole room cheering,
and I don't know how this happens next,
but I get up on this stool and I start making these *orations,* first about…
Sex: the mysteries and the cult of the clitoris:
high priests, low priests,
knee-deep shit:
I talk about black out orgasms, biting,
transcendental leg spasms.
I can't really remember all the shit I'm talking about, but
it's somewhere in the middle of all this that Hannah walks in,
her lips still dried out from earlier.
I can tell that people are still listening, like,
they think this is a dramatic pause or something,
but really I'm just *stuck…*

    (beat)

How do you explain *this?*
How do you explain that you share something with someone that nobody can touch, that nobody can buy or control, that yesterday wasn't even on your radar?
I want to talk about love, but

what the fuck do I say?
I get everyone to finish their drinks.
I fucking love you all very much.
That's it for speeches.

>   *(beat)*
>
>   *(light shift)*

The power goes out after midnight; candles are lit.
People are worried about staying out past curfew,
but I coax a small group into staying by getting the owner to call for coke.
I told you I spent every dime and it didn't matter because soon the rain would stop and I would die…

>   *(sound of rain falling)*
>
>   *(beat)*

It felt so sweet.
I wasn't scared.
Honest.
Every moment contained so much.
It was like back at the bomb site, the way I could see and feel everything:
the people moving beside me, their gestures, their conversations;
the clock on the wall, the bartender tipping a bottle;
Hannah rubbing my hand, her dry lips moving,
every cough, dropped word, laugh, sniff—
all pouring into this constant flow of moments where *nothing was missing.*
I smoke as Hannah talks.
She talks about her growing up in the camps,
not having a home until she's sixteen, the strangeness of a city,
living with people of no common past—
And yeah, I got carried away and maybe said some things I shouldn't have said.

But I was *engaged*, you know?
The coke,
the alcohol,
Her.

    (beat)

We talk and we talk til' the candles burn down to their last sad stumps,
alone at the bar, bartender passed out in a booth,
light outside, still raining, like,
a drizzle.

    (Rain quiets down.)

We walk home and
when we get back to her place she tells me she's making coffee,
but she falls asleep while the water is boiling, and
It's *barely* raining now, I mean,
I can *just* make out those little drops on the puddles.
I take off the kettle.

    (beat)

Hannah, I didn't mean to do this.
I curl myself up next her and the last thing I hear is her heart beating.

    (beat)

    (rain intensifies)

    (light shift)

At ten thirty Hannah tells me she's going to work. She tells me I can stay.
Not a lot happens in the next couple of days.
It rains. I'm in Hannah's pocket so I wait around the house a lot.
She asks me why I don't go anywhere.
I don't know what to tell her.
At the same time it's great to be around her

— I fuckin' love her, but I feel like she starts looking at me differently now that
I'm around the house all the time and not particularly doing anything...
And t*oo much* time alone, you know...?
I start to doubt things:
"Listen, Hannah, I've been doing a lot of thinking. Maybe we should stop doing this. Because if we don't, like, maybe one of us is going to get hurt."

    (beat)

"Hannah, you know, I'm really fucked up right now. I'm not making any sense. I think it'd be best if we just..."

    (beat)

I *tried* to end it, but it shouldn't have been like pulling teeth!

    (lighting change)

One morning we're sitting together,
I'm reading the paper and I see that...
they're having my funeral!
I figure that maybe — hey — maybe *this* is a good opportunity to, you know,
explain to her.
Plus, tell me which of you would not, given the chance, attend your own funeral?
Of course I'm attending that shit. So I tell her, I say,
"Hannah, this dear dear friend of mine has passed away recently.
See, it's part of why I've been so messed up"
— which, if you think about it, is actually kind of true—
and I ask her if she'd like to come.
She says yes.

    (beat)

    (light shift)

This is at the rec centre:

White flowers, vodka, simple wood coffin.
Part of me really wants to peek inside the coffin but
I hang back because everywhere there are these people who know me, and,
it's crazy, man, not just the *good people*...
even the *biggest assholes:*
my mom's sister, her husband;
those rats who used to hang out near the tennis court—
Everyone acting real respectful.
Somehow in all this Hannah is chill:
We watch the preacher climbing up on his small stage, and
he preaches his bit, which, okay, I get, but
he's saying all the *Christian things*, like
"she is in heaven" or "with our father",
and I'm thinking, like,
Jesus,
what the fuck does this man know about death?
I want to go up there and tell them all what it's like.
I want to tell them about turning into water or being pulled apart by air.
I want them to know that it's fine, really. But...
It's a feeling: even if I could tell them...
then what?

    (beat)

It starts to bug me.
I wonder whether anyone got the message on the backside of the school.
So I go up into the bathrooms,
boys and girls,
I hit up every urinal, every stall.
I write in *my* letters
"Seabird is in a Happy Place" "Seabird is in a Happy Place" "Seabird is in a Happy Place"
'cept this time I don't feel any better doing it.

> *(beat)*

I come back and Hannah is over at the coffin checkin'
out this picture of me — this...
twelfth grade picture.
I'm in a white dress
— the only time I ever wear a white dress!
My mom comes up to her and
The two of them start talking.
They don't talk for long,
but they're talking as though they know each other.
When they're done they hug, and
Hannah comes back over.
I ask her, what she was talking about. She says
"it's none of your business."
None of my business? She says
"Seabird, it wouldn't be polite".
And I'm like,
"It's my fucking mother, you bitch!"
But I say this way too loud.

> *(beat)*

Everybody *knows* it's me!
and still Hannah is leading me out of the rec centre,
her hand in mine,
getting me on a bus and we're going back to her place,
and when we get there neither of us feel like talking
so we just sit on the couch and listen to this piano tape
she has and—

> *(Sound of piano playing — something soft, a crackle over the audio.)*

What the fuck am I crying for?
It's my own fuckin' funeral!
But it feels so good to cry next to her.
And on this tape I notice there's a crackling like
it was raining when the piano was recorded, and
Hannah says to me,

"You're going to die, Seabird.
You're going to die and you're going to leave me here."
And
I want to tell her it isn't true, but
she's right.

> *(Sound of crackling, overcomes the piano music, transitions to sound of raining, rain mounts until it is indecipherable from a herd of stampeding horses.)*

> *(light shift.)*

I'll go through the last four days, real quickly.
It kept on raining, obviously.
The levees broke on the eastside so most of downtown flooded.
Hannah lived on the far edge of the flooding so we only had to splash thru a couple inches while dudes in the flood zone had to, like, swim through their kitchen.
The military declared a state of emergency.
On the second day they started evacuation of the eastside.
There was going to be a meeting in Hannah's neighbourhood to determine whether or not people could stay in their homes, but by the time of the meeting the hall had flooded so…
We didn't get to choose.
We followed the military across town to a rally point in Governor's Park and
waited under a band shell for a bunch of school buses to pick us up.

> *(beat)*

It was not where we wanted to be,
in a camp.
Everybody knew about the shitty living conditions
— like they were designed off the interior of some military prick's asshole.
On top of that, there was water pooling everywhere

which made a lot of people nervous, because they knew that was how sickness spread.

Hannah and I shared a mat in a room full of mostly women.

On the third day I get sick.

It isn't bad, but what the fuck?

I had been blown up and put back together and

now I'm suffering from diarrhea?

Fuck off.

I don't eat anything that day and by the time I feel good enough to move I've missed most of the last meal.

One of the wardens tells me they're still serving a couple emplacements down so I go out to get some.

I don't tell Hannah where I'm going because I figure I'll be back right away.

But I don't come back.

After I get dinner, I get lost.

Every building looks the same, and with the lights off and the people sleeping inside, there was just no fucking way…

I ask one of the wardens if she can look up some information for me,

but she tells me that the names on her list have yet to be paired to residencies;

I'll have to wait til' morning.

She shows me to a room where there are a couple spare mattresses.

(beat)

This is the first night I spend without Hannah and what do I care — but I miss her.

I mean, I actually can't sleep without her.

And what if something happens to her while I'm not there, you know?

What if some freak sees her sleeping alone? What will he do to her?

And it just—

>   *(beat)*

All of this is my fault.

>   *(beat)*
>
>   *(light shift)*

The next morning I'm sick again.
This time, worse. I wake up puking. The meds examine me.
They recommend isolation. I tell them,
"Listen, there's someone I really need to see,
who doesn't know where I am, who is probably pretty fucking scared…"
But it's not happening.
They shoot me up with something like, liquid sunshine, like really good stuff,
and it's already in that moment I can feel myself turning into air again.
I feel myself forgetting…
about the flood,
about Hannah,
about everything.

>   *(beat)*

It's stopped raining.

>   *(light shift)*

They transfer me to this room.
It's not a room but, like,
a bath tub with shower curtains all around it and
I don't know if I'm hallucinating,
but I can hear people on the other side of the curtain and
somehow I know that these people are dead, all of them.

Everyone on the other side of the curtain is dead and I'm alive.
I don't know where Hannah is.
I don't want to see Hannah, but I want to tell her that I'm okay.
I want to write to her in my letters
"Seabird is in a happy place",
which is sad because it isn't even true any more.
What's true is that I'm sitting here dying in luxury
while I've left her to this bitch of a world by herself.
It isn't fair.

The Gulf

Audrey Cefaly

THE GULF first premiered in August of 2010 as part of the Silver Spring Stage One-Act Festival. The production was directed by Chris Curtis. The cast was as follows:

BETTY . . . . Erika Imhoof
KENDRA . . . . Audrey Cefaly

THE GULF was subsequently produced as part of the Samuel French Off Off Broadway Short Play Festival at the East 13th Street Theatre in New York City on August 9, 2015. The prodcution was directed by Joseph Holmgren. Scenic design was by Nicole Allan. The Stage Manager was Emma Ruopp. The cast was as follows:

BETTY . . . . Effie Johnson
KENDRA . . . . Carolyn Messina

CHARACTERS

BETTY – 20s-40s. An optimist. A thinker. Restless and tender-hearted.

KENDRA – 20s-40s. A woman of few words. A loner. Scrappy, dark, brutish and volatile.

SETTING

Present day. A fishing boat. Alabama delta.

-

(On a quiet summer evening, somewhere down in the Alabama Delta, **KENDRA** *and* **BETTY** *troll the flats looking for redfish.)*

*(***KENDRA** *slowly reels in the line while* **BETTY** *lies with her feet in* **KENDRA***'s lap, reading* What Color is Your Parachute: A Practical Manual for Job-Hunters and Career Changers. **KENDRA** *sighs…)*

BETTY. What?

KENDRA. Nothin' but rats.

BETTY. Huh?

KENDRA. Man…some *scrawny* rat reds tonight…

BETTY. Kinda bait are you using?

KENDRA. Baby, if the fish ain't bitin it ain't cuz of the bait. It's cuz they ain't there.

BETTY. Wan' go somewhere else?

KENDRA. Nope.

BETTY. Rosella was talking about over by Bottle Creek.

KENDRA. Bottle Creek?

BETTY. I told her we were comin' out here.

(beat)

She was bein' helpful.

KENDRA. Rosella has no idea about fishin' and therefore Rosella is not helpful.

BETTY. What's wrong with Bottle Creek? Can't fish in Bottle Creek?

KENDRA. Yeah, for boots and dead bodies.

BETTY. I thought there was good fishin' there.

KENDRA. Well there was, but not no more.

BETTY. How come?

KENDRA. BP Fuckers.

BETTY. BP?

KENDRA. That shit got in…choked it.

BETTY. Aw shit…

> *(beat)*

You know…you got the whole Gulf of Mexico to fish in, we always end up here.

KENDRA. What are you sayin'?

BETTY. Right here in the shallows, every time.

KENDRA. That's the whole point.

BETTY. I don't get it.

KENDRA. Exactly.

BETTY. What?

KENDRA. That's where the — nevermind.

BETTY. No, tell me. Please.

KENDRA. Fish in the shallows, cuz that's where the fish are.

> *(beat)*

Reds like to fight, Betty, they fight…deep, shallow, whatever, any water. But in the shallows, they get more traction, see, the fight is bigger…more fun.

BETTY. For you, maybe.

> *(beat)*

KENDRA. When did you talk to Rosella?

BETTY. Last night…

> *(beat)*

It's warm, idn't it? I might hop in for a swim if I didn't think the gators would get me.

KENDRA. Assuming they'd want you.

> **(BETTY** *returns to reading her book.)*

BETTY. *(off* **KENDRA***'s look)* What?

KENDRA. Nothin'.

BETTY. Why can't I do what I want to do? You're doin' your thing.

KENDRA. Fishin' boat, not a library.

BETTY. I could fish if I wanted to, I ain't in the mood.

> *(beat)*

I know how to fish. I do!

KENDRA. When did you ever fish?

BETTY. When I was little. Caught my first fish when I was eight years old. It counts! It does! Stop it, stop laughin'.

KENDRA. What'd you catch?

BETTY. Sunfish.

KENDRA. Sunfish?

BETTY. Little ole Sunfish. Daddy said to me, now Betty, the rule is…you catch it, you gotta clean it. And then I found out what cleaning was and I thought I don't want to have nothin' to do with that.

KENDRA. So what'd you do?

BETTY. I just put him in the well, there, under the boat… laid there watchin' him. I can't do it. I can't do what you do. You…gut those fish wide open like it's nothin'. That catfish last week, his little heart just floppin' all over the boat, why you reckon it does that?

> *(beat)*

You caught that fish, took out the *insides,* the heart is just layin' there, it's still beatin', Kendra. The fuck… why'st do that?

KENDRA. *(playfully)* Cuz it loves me. Even in death it loves me. It's what I got, I can't help it.

> *(beat)*

So what'd you do with him?

BETTY. Who?

KENDRA. Sunfish.

BETTY. Oh…umn… I just picked him up by his tail and put him back in the water. He didn't move none at first, he just laid there, like he was dead or somethin. I put my little finger on him and he made a ruckus and swam off. Back to his family.

KENDRA. *Back to his family.*

BETTY. His family — whatever — you're bein mean!

KENDRA. I ain't bein' mean. You always think I'm bein 'mean, I'm just listenin'.

>   *(beat)*

BETTY. *Whatever.*

KENDRA. Oh here we go…look at this asshole…

BETTY. Who is it?

KENDRA. Oh, my god. Will you look at that? What kinda dumbass comes out to fish the flats in a shit-tub like that…

>   (**KENDRA** *tries to make out whose boat it is.*)
>
>   *(calling)*

Duke?! What the fuck are you drivin' man, you just got paid or what? Oh, I'm sure the fish love it, they be floatin' up dead at the sight of it.

>   *(to* **BETTY***)*

Stupid fuck.

>   *(to Duke)*

Man…you know what? You can make fun of my coon-ass boat package all you want, but we'll see who's up by the end of the night, won't we? You should try up by Bottle Creek…

BETTY. *(overlapping)* Kendra!

KENDRA. *(continuing)* Oh, hell yeah. Redfish, gars, trout, whatever, fulla surprises, that Bottle Creek.

>   *(beat)*

Would I lie to you? Move along Duke, you're spookin' my fish…

>   *(to* **BETTY***)*

Say goodbye Betty.

(They lazily shoot the bird at Duke as his boat rides by. **KENDRA** *notices Thelma in the back of the boat.)*

(to Thelma)

Hey Thelma!

*(**KENDRA** turns to see that **BETTY** has pulled out a small picnic basket and is assembling some fancy fixings for a snack.)*

What the fuck is that?

BETTY. *(defensively)* This is all the same food that you eat every other day of the week, only today it is newly configured into this creative combination for our little fishing excursion.

KENDRA. You gon' answer my question?

BETTY. Tapanade.

KENDRA. *Tapanade.*

BETTY. Olive tapanade. Garlic, capers, basil, lemon. All chopped up.

KENDRA. OK, so…olives?

(They glare at each other, as if in a stand-off. **BETTY** *holds up another option…)*

BETTY. Canapé.

KENDRA. That is not a can-a-paint or whatever the fuck word you're sayin', that there is a Ritz cracker with some kind of bullshit green distraction, something like a Vienna *(pron: Vai-yee-ner)* sausage and a snot drop of Cheez Whiz on top.

BETTY. Snot drop? That's disgusting.

(beat)

Are you serious right now? You know what, you remind me of like some kinda Neanderthal cave man except without any of the social skills. Actually, I take that back. You are like a Neanderthal cave man with just enough social skills to kind of blend into your *sewage plant* surroundings, but I would say even that is a little bit of a stretch.

(beat)

Hello?

*(**KENDRA** busily digs into the cooler for another beer.)*

I don't even know why I bother…

*(**BETTY** starts packing up the food.)*

…try to educate you…broaden your horizons, and you are basically a 12-year-old boy.

(beat)

What are you doing?

KENDRA. *(busily doing something else)* I am over here not giving a fuck about anything coming out of your mouth.

(beat)

BETTY. Do you listen to yourself when you talk? Do you hear the things you say or—you know what, forget it.

*(**BETTY** begins to pack the food back up.)*

For the record, Kendra…that there is andouille sausage, or maybe you've heard of it, *arugula* and fucking aged Wisconsin cheddar, which looks nothing like the barbaric mutation that is Cheez Whiz. Because A, it's not melted, and B, it's just sitting there, not melted. If it was Cheez Whiz—which it NEVER WILL BE—it would look a little different, now wouldn't it? It would look—

KENDRA. *(overlapping — deadpan)* Like a snot blob?

(beat)

BETTY. You see me here holding this piece of cheese, Kendra? This is my kryptonite. I am immune to you and all of your mean-spirited mental terroristics.

*(**BETTY** pops the piece of cheese into her mouth, staring at **KENDRA** defiantly as she chews it.)*

KENDRA. That's your kryptonite?

BETTY. Yep.

KENDRA. You're ingesting your own kryptonite?

BETTY. Yep.

KENDRA. Just checkin'.

BETTY. *(regarding the cheese)* God-DAMN that's good.

*(**BETTY** pulls out her book and resumes reading.)*

(beat)

KENDRA. Oh, good. That's good. Let's read a book. Let's all read a book.

BETTY. *(reading aloud) Theoretically, you could be just as happy as a garbage collector.*

*(to **KENDRA**)*

They have the least amount of stress as any job, you know that? I read that someplace. And think about it. What do they have to be stressed about anyway, except maybe, you know, some maggots and dead rats and whatnot?

KENDRA. I don't know.

BETTY. And you know what… I bet after a couple weeks even the maggots would just be routine, whaddya reckon? Alright, now here is a list of possible occupations, however, this is in no way — here it says — *no way intended to be a definitive list, but more a list of suggestions based upon your core competencies and desires.*

(beat)

I'll just read the list.

KENDRA. *(seriously annoyed)* Please.

BETTY. *(reading)* Prison guard.

(beat)

KENDRA. *Prison guard?*

BETTY. Yep.

KENDRA. *(incredulous)* You added my whole life up on that worksheet there and that's what came out?

BETTY. I may have added a few ideas of my own.

KENDRA. Like prison guard…

BETTY. Yeah, like prison guard yes, like a lotta things, are you gonna keep an open mind or maybe we'll just quit all this, how bout that? This book *helped me*, K. It's how come I know what I wanna be now, and before I was just driftin around and whatnot.

KENDRA. Good for you.

(beat)

BETTY. Are you jealous of me?

KENDRA. *(increasingly frustrated)* Could we be more different? I wonder.

BETTY. Well, what does that mean?

KENDRA. Look, this is *your dream*, not mine, this *social working* whatever, and I want you to go to school. I do. I'm proud of you…

BETTY. *(overlapping)* Why won't you come with me?

KENDRA. We have been through this.

BETTY. It's junior college, not forever.

KENDRA. Exactly.

BETTY. Well, I don't like the idea of us bein' apart, do you? Hello?

KENDRA. What?

BETTY. You gotta see the world sometime. What are you gonna do, fish the rest of your life?

KENDRA. Well, I don't know, is it on the list? Why do I need a parachute, anyway? What the fuck is that?

BETTY. It's not an *actual* parachute.

KENDRA. Just a pretend parachute.

BETTY. It's a *metaphor*. Do you remember me tellin' you that about 20 minutes ago?

KENDRA. Uh… I think I'd remember a pretend parachute.

BETTY. Well, I guess so, especially when you're stuck somewhere WITHOUT IT!

> *(digging in)*

Welder. Mechanic. Dairy Queen Manager. That was a test…to see if you were listenin', are you listenin?

KENDRA. *(overlapping)* Yes, god, yes!

BETTY. Wedding planner.

KENDRA. Fuck off!

BETTY. Mortician.

> *(beat)*

What?

KENDRA. *Mortician?*

BETTY. You can thank me for that one.

KENDRA. Mortician?

BETTY. Only because I know how much you like dead people.

> (**KENDRA** *stares at* **BETTY** *as if she has three heads.*)

That's how come you watch that show all the time, with the "Y" incision.

KENDRA. Dr. G —

> *(beat)*

*Dr. G…*is not a mortician, Betty. Dr. G is a medical examiner for the city of Orlando — that's a good one, actually, medical examiner, write that down — and I don't watch that show for the dead people, okay, I told you that.

BETTY. *(playfully)* Have you got a crush on Dr. G?

KENDRA. Just write it down!

> (**BETTY** *freezes for a moment, retracing their steps.*)

BETTY. Oh, shoot. I got that kryptonite thing backwards, huh?

KENDRA. Yep.

BETTY. Shit.

(BETTY *notices* KENDRA'*s knife laying nearby. She picks it up and turns it over in her hands, caressing the blade.* KENDRA *is wildly aroused by this…*)

KENDRA. You gon' cut me open?

BETTY. I was thinkin' about it…

KENDRA. Let's do it.

BETTY. *(staring at the blade)* How long does a fish heart keep beatin'after you…ya know…

KENDRA. 3.2 seconds.

BETTY. 3.2 seconds?

KENDRA. I don't know Betty! I never counted, Jesus Chist with the fish hearts!!

BETTY. Don't be mean.

KENDRA. I'm not bein' mea —— stop trippin' —— give me the knife!

    (beat)

I want you to stop thinking.

BETTY. Why?

KENDRA. Because when you think, I'm miserable!

BETTY. Why won't you think about it? You been sayin' you need a change, you been sayin' you hate it here.

KENDRA. It's just talk.

BETTY. No it ain't.

KENDRA. It's only 100 miles away, Betty. What's the big deal anyway?

BETTY. Well it just seems to me you ain't happy and maybe this could be a shot at something different, something good.

KENDRA. Could we move on, please, to some topic I give a shit about? I ain't gon' choose my calling offa some list you got from a self-help book.

BETTY. This is a career-path *workbook*, Kendra. What color is *your* parachute?

KENDRA. Red.

BETTY. It is not red. It is not at all red, and if you had been listenin', you would know that. We are on chapter nine, Kendra. *Geography of the Heart.*

KENDRA. Is that the last chapter? I sure hope it is.

BETTY. *(overlapping)* You are being obtuse.

KENDRA. Absolutely, I'm being obtuse—

BETTY. *(overlapping)* Do you even know what that means —

KENDRA. I would *love* to know what that means!

BETTY. It means somebody who is smarter than hell, but who is set on pretending to be *dumber than shit* so maybe nothing is ever expected of 'em and then they don't have to do anything but sit around and fish for all eternity. How's that sound?

KENDRA. *(beat)* Is that a trick question?

BETTY. Do you have a plan? For your future?

KENDRA. Will you stop?

BETTY. Do you?

KENDRA. I had a plan. Yeah. I had a plan to do a little drum fishin', maybe catch a bull red or two and not have to deal with ridiculous questions and psychotic-analysis, how's that for a plan?!

BETTY. *(overlapping)* I will never understand you.

KENDRA. Thank GOD for that!

BETTY. Open…your mind!

KENDRA. To what?

BETTY. The future.

KENDRA. I have a job.

BETTY. That's not a job…

    (beat)

You work at a sewage plant.

KENDRA. Oh, and your job is saving lives, I guess. Is that it?

BETTY. Well, yeah, actually, it is, if you wanna know. I do save a life from time to time. Jenny Pelligrin gave me some of her nitro pills to keep under the bar, just yesterday afternoon, in case she ever goes into cardiac arrest. I keep a box of condoms under there, Trojans... for Bobby Lee, right next to the margarita mix and the rock salt. Swear to god, it's a damn pharmacy under there. You wouldn't believe the shit I see. These folks, they come in there...half of 'em want to get laid, half of 'em want to get drunk and the other half just need to talk. And it ain't in my job description, but I do it, cuz that's what bartenders do...they listen. I listen to 'em and you know what I hear?

    (beat)

Desperation. Quiet desperation. So quiet, only dogs can hear. In the eyes, the shaky voice. Starin' down at the ice cubes in the glass, like readin' tea leaves or some shit. I pour 'em one on the house, I look 'em square in the eye, and I ask 'em the same thing I'm askin' you.

    (beat)

Oh, come on K, can't you open your mind and think about it.

I mean is it really that hard to imagine? No, seriously. If you could be anything at all in the whole wide world, what would it be?

KENDRA. Alone.

BETTY. Oh, shut up. You couldn't be alone no more than I could. You can't even sleep with the light off.

KENDRA. I'm afraid of the dark now, is that it?

BETTY. Afraid of somethin'...

KENDRA. *(overlapping)* Oh my god!

BETTY. You sleep with the light on...you fish in the shallows...

KENDRA. And you speak Chinese, the fuck are you talking about? I'm...I'm afraid to live or some shit?

BETTY. Maybe. Maybe you are.

KENDRA. And you don't know how to sit still, how about that? Nothing's ever good enough for you, is it? We came out here to *fish*. But you never fish, Betty.

BETTY. Yes, I do.

KENDRA. *(overlapping)* You don't. And you don't want to learn, either, you just want to sit there with your books and your papers and whatnot, and rearrange *my life* to make it fit yours in some magical futuristic happy place that exists — where? I don't know, in your mind, maybe? Meanwhile, I'm doin' it. I'm taking part in the miraculousness of life, Betty. REAL LIFE. Where folks catch fish, rip their FUCKING guts out and then eat 'em. And they don't think twice about it and you wanna know why? Cuz it's just FISHIN'!

BETTY. Do you love me?

KENDRA. *(a warning)* I'm 'on lose it.

BETTY. Do you?

> *(inching closer and closer to **KENDRA**)*

Sex ed teacher…underwear model…massage therapist.

KENDRA. Yes. I love you.

BETTY. I love you too.

> *(They kiss. **KENDRA** pulls open the folds of **BETTY**'s blouse to kiss her neck…)*

KENDRA. You smell like roses…

BETTY. Mmn…

KENDRA. Wait.

BETTY. God I love you.

KENDRA. What is that?

BETTY. What?

KENDRA. What is that smell?

> *(beat)*

I fuckin' knew it.

BETTY. K…

KENDRA. You been up to Butler county, hadn't you? You been up there with her? And now you're sittin here with me, parachute bullshit trying to straighten out my fucking life. That is some fantastic shit.

BETTY. I was putting an end to it.

KENDRA. In person? God. FUCK! I'm such an asshole.
BETTY. It's not what you think.
KENDRA. *(mimicking) I've changed, K, I've changed.*
BETTY. I have.
KENDRA. Oh, please. You are still the same slut I met at Mardi Gras.
BETTY. Yeah, well you took to it pretty quick as I recall.
KENDRA. What are you gonna do, Betty?
BETTY. About what?
KENDRA. *About your fucking life!* You can't keep that shit locked up for two seconds? Howlin' all over town like some bitch in heat. And you stink too, Betty, by the way. You need some feminine hygiene. All our time together, six years I gave you, took you back, took the BITCH back, WHY? Why the fuck did I — junior college?! I'm gon' pack up my shit and go with you to junior college?! That is fuckin hilarious. I'm done. I am beyond done.

> (**KENDRA** *grabs* **BETTY***'s backpack.* **BETTY** *reaches to take it from her.*)

LEAVE IT! Leave it.

> *(menacing)*

Get outta the boat.
BETTY. K…
KENDRA. Get. Out. Of the boat.

> *(beat)*

What?! What the hell do you want from me? Can't you tell I hate you? Can't you tell I hate your fat ass?!
BETTY. No you don't.
KENDRA. Oh, I do! I do! You are killin' me. I want you to go. I want you to just get your shit and go… PLEASE. I can't do this no more. You wanna know the truth? I'm glad you're leavin'. I been wantin' you to leave since July! You are bad for me…you are bad for my soul, Betty.

(**KENDRA** *starts throwing* **BETTY**'*s things overboard.*)

BETTY. K, please, stop, stop…

KENDRA. Out…get out…out, out, out…

BETTY. K! I love you!

(**KENDRA** *looks at* **BETTY** *a moment and then violently pushes her overboard.*)

KENDRA. OUT!

(**KENDRA** *grabs whatever she can find and begins throwing it all at* **BETTY** *who is floundering in the shallows behind the boat.*)

OUT, out, out!!!! And take this psycho-shit with you. Maybe there's a chapter in there about skanks and the morons that love 'em.

(**KENDRA** *throws the book overboard.*)

Where's that parachute now, BITCH?! That ought to break ya, huh? Egg-suckin' dog.

(**KENDRA** *collapses exhausted into a heap inside the boat.*)

Damn Betty. You wear me out!

(*long silence*)

(*The soaking wet book flies back into the boat.* **KENDRA** *remains motionless. A hand reaches up and grabs the side of the boat, then another, then a foot, as* **BETTY** *crawls back in.*)

(*silence*)

BETTY. Kendra…

KENDRA. (*a lifeless syllable*) Hmn…

BETTY. I think maybe you have some pent-up hostility toward me.

KENDRA. How'd you guess that?

BETTY. I'm sorry, K.

KENDRA. *(a whisper)* Why do you do it?

BETTY. What?

KENDRA. Why do you do it?

BETTY. I wish I knew. I ain't never been any other way. I could never understand it myself 'til that time my cousin told me I had codependence. And then I started to think on it and that's when I realized maybe she was right 'cuz it did seem like I had somethin' wrong with me to where I always needed somebody, you know, like the thought of being by myself was…do you hate me?

KENDRA. *(numb)* Yeah.

> *(Childlike,* **BETTY** *rather shakily situates herself in the boat and leans back to look up at the night sky.)*

BETTY. One fish, two fish, red fish, blue fish. This one has a little star, this one has a little car, say what a lot of fish there are.

> *(beat)*

You ever sit and think about your life in reverse…like back to that second when it was all just exactly the way you dreamt it could be?

KENDRA. No.

BETTY. You walked into the Judge Roy Bean's on Fat Tuesday. 'Member that ? I was sittin' there at the bar and I looked up and saw you…holy shit. Leather jacket…snake-skin boots. 30 pounds of Mardi Gras beads hanging off that rack of yours. How's you get all them beads anyway?

KENDRA. Offa some Baylor boys…

BETTY. Baylor?

KENDRA. I just went up to a group of Baylor boys and I asked real nice.

BETTY. What you say?

KENDRA. Hand 'em over.

BETTY. And they just gave 'em up, huh. Just like that.

KENDRA. Yep.

BETTY. Out of the kindness of their hearts.

KENDRA. *(overlapping)* Yep.

BETTY. You had your tits out didn't ya?

KENDRA. All the way out.

BETTY. You flashed 'em good, didn't ya? I'm surprised they didn't go blind.

KENDRA. Few of 'em did.

BETTY. That was it for me. That night. I know I'd never love nobody like you. And I hadn't. All these years.

KENDRA. I just wish I was enough.

BETTY. You are.

KENDRA. You are so ridiculous.

BETTY. What?

KENDRA. That's the difference between us. You ain't never gon' be happy with me.

BETTY. I —

KENDRA. No. Face it.

> *(beat)*

We gotta go…

BETTY. Go where?

> **(BETTY** *touches* **KENDRA**'s *hand…)*

You've always had the prettiest hands…

> *(beat)*

I feel like we're disappearin'…

KENDRA. Sssshhh. Let's just sit here for a while. Tide starts movin'…we'll catch a few.

> *(beat)*

I'm sorry about what I said…

BETTY. About what?

KENDRA. Feminine hygiene.

BETTY. Oh.

KENDRA. You smell good to me.

(beat)

BETTY. 3.2 seconds…

KENDRA. I just made that up.

BETTY. I know you did. But…how long, though. If you had to guess…how long before it stops.

KENDRA. Maybe a minute…*(beat)*

BETTY. A whole minute? Wow. Does it just stop or does it slow down and then stop.

KENDRA. Slows down a bit.

BETTY. Why does it do that…

KENDRA. What's that?

BETTY. Why does it keep beating like that…

(beat)

KENDRA. Habit.

(silence)

*(**KENDRA** drinks down the last drop of her beer and tosses her can into the corner of the boat. She casts her line once more into the shallows. **BETTY** opens her book and reads aloud.)*

BETTY. *Pet psychic. Meter maid. Dental hygienist.*

Throws of Love

Amy Staats

THROWS OF LOVE was first written and performed as part of Sacramento City College's 29 1/2 Hour Playwriting Festival in September 2005. It was directed by James Roberts. The cast was as follows:

MRS. BRAUGHMER .... Kim McCann-Lawson
LINDY .... Midori Iwata
JENNY .... Michelle Murphy
NORA .... Janet Ma

THROWS OF LOVE was subsequently produced in New York City at The Barrow Group Theatre as part of Core Ensemble's Twisted Shorts from October 17, 2014 to October 27, 2014. The production was directed by Rachel Casparian. The Director of Production was Farrah Crane, and the Stage Manager was Kacey Gritters. Music was by Adam Platt, with lighting by Sean Gorski, costume consultation by Eddie James, fight direction by Ron Piretti, and magic consultation by Jeffery Kellogg. The cast was as follows:

MRS. BRAUGHMER .... Catherine Curtin
LINDY .... Kara Dudley
JENNY .... Katie Lawson
NORA .... Nathalie Frederick

THROWS OF LOVE was produced as part of the Samuel French Off Off Broadway Short Play Festival at the East 13th Street Theatre in New York City on August 9, 2015. The production was directed by Jess Chayes. The producers were Amy Staats and Megan Hill. The Stage Manager: was Samantha Gruskin, with fight choreography by Ron Piretti. The cast was as follows:

MRS. BRAUGHMER .... Catherine Curtin
LINDY .... Kara Dudley
JENNY .... Katie Lawson
NORA .... Bindu Bansinath

CHARACTERS

MRS. BRAUGHMER – 40s, former girl scout leader. Grieving
LINDY – 13, in love with Jimmy
JENNY – 13, in love with Jimmy
NORA – 13, not in love with Jimmy

SETTING

Suburban neighborhood in Sacramento, California

TIME

Present day - 2am

AUTHOR'S NOTES

The comedy in this play works best when it is played very truthfully and the stakes are high.

PROP NOTES

This play works well without a full set, as long as you have the props. The throwing of the toilet paper is very theatrical and fun to see on stage. Also, it's exciting if you actually throw an egg at the end. (It's possible to make cleanable prop eggs. Google Prop: Throwable Eggs. I recommend the one where you blow out the egg, fill it with gelatin, and seal it with wax paper and glue.)

(Front yard of a two story suburban house: 2AM. **LINDY**, **JENNY** *and* **NORA** *[all 13] sneak up to the bushes on the side of the lawn and hide behind them. They are wearing pajamas and carry flashlights and a homemade sign that says "We Love Jimmy". They stare up at a second floor window.)*

LINDY. Oh my God, that's his room.

JENNY. Where?

NORA. I still don't see how this is going to help.

LINDY. On the left…

JENNY. Oh my God. Right. Remember at the party?

LINDY. Yeah. Yeah. Oh my God. He was so fine…

JENNY. He *is* so fine.

LINDY. I love him.

JENNY. Me too.

LINDY. Yeah but…

JENNY. What?

LINDY. Nothing. Nevermind.

(They pass around a bottle of peppermint schnapps.)

NORA. You guys…are you sure? My Mom says we're too young to fall in love. It's temporary. Like the feeling you get when using cocaine or methamphetamines.

JENNY. Really?

LINDY. No way. *I love him.*

JENNY. Me too.

*(**LINDY** *and* **JENNY** *pull multiple rolls of toilet paper out of* **NORA***'s backpack and start TPing the house.* **LINDY** *places the "We Love Jimmy" sign*

under the window. **MRS. BRAUGHMER** *calls out from inside the house.*)

MRS B. Hey...

LINDY & JENNY. Shit.

MRS B. Stop that! What are you doing? Lindy? Lindy, is that you? Don't you dare move a muscle.

(**LINDY** *freezes, caught.* **JENNY** *and* **NORA** *scurry under the bushes.* **MRS. BRAUGHMER** *enters in her robe carrying a beer.*)

I'm going to speak to your father! I'm going to... Goddammit. Oh shit. It's all in the roses.

Two in the goddamn morning.

(**MRS. BRAUGHMER** *starts pulling down toilet paper and notices the "We love Jimmy" sign. She picks it up, sits on the front steps and starts to cry.*)

LINDY. Um... Mrs. Braughmer?

MRS B. Lindy Kramer. Where do you get off throwing fucking toilet paper all over our goddamn lawn? This is private property ya know.

LINDY. Um...

MRS B. I could call the cops. You could get arrested. I was your Girl Scout leader for God's sake.

LINDY. I know. I'm sorry. I...

MRS B. I gave you your fucking civic responsibility badge. You aughta be ashamed of yourself. Now... I'm gonna sit here with my beer and watch you pick all of this up.

LINDY. Okay. Please don't tell my father.

MRS B. Well...we'll see about that. You think its gonna be easy getting toilet paper out of my roses? Poor thing, you're gonna get all pricked up. Huh. Yeah.

(**MRS B** *watches* **LINDY** *pick the toilet paper out of the rose bushes. She drinks.*)

So... You love Jimmy, huh?

LINDY. Well...um...

MRS B. Couldn't ya just have called or sent him a note or something?

LINDY. Um…

MRS B. He's not even here. He's at Nicholas's house. You should of tried over there. Maybe his mother would appreciate the decoration.

LINDY. Um…

MRS B. You're lucky Mr. Braughmer isn't home. Very lucky. He could be here any minute…he could… Oh God. Look at you. You're thirteen years old. You're a child. What a you doin' falling in love?

LINDY. Mrs. Braughmer, are you okay?

MRS B. Me? Well… I'm a little drunk I guess. I guess I may be a little drunk. I bet you've never seen me this way. I bet you never…

LINDY. Um…

MRS B. Yoo-hoo girls! Come on out. Come to the party.

*(**NORA** and **JENNY** come out of the bushes.)*

NORA. Um…

MRS B. Oh Nora… I am surprised. Not at you Jenny. Give it.

*(**JENNY** hands **MRS. BRAUGHMER** the Schnapps.)*

You… I am not surprised at all. But Nora…well well well.

JENNY. We should go. Curfew? The cops?

(Nobody moves.)

MRS B. Cops?

*(**MRS. BRAUGHMER** takes a swig.)*

Ugh. Terrible. Don't worry. I'll tell 'em we're having a Girl Scout meeting. Night project. Slugs. *(indicates beer)* Organic pest control. You put it in a little saucer and those slugs just drink it up. And then they drown. Right in their own drink. Right in a puddle of suds. What a way to die.

NORA. Do you think that slugs feel pain?

MRS B. I don't know Nora. I do not know. Maybe they feel a panic, like something's happening that's not quite right, but hey, they're having a good time, so maybe it's okay. But then there's that little voice that thinks… maybe everything's not okay. And may be that little voice knows something that the big voice isn't ready to know. But I suppose on some level they know they're being fucked over. And this time, well…they're gonna have to do something about it. If they can just…get themselves out of the goddamn saucer.

> *(They girls stare at **MRS. BRAUGHMER**. **MRS. BRAUGHMER** stares at the girls. She drinks, alternating Schnapps with beer.)*

LINDY. Um…

MRS B. Not a pretty sight, huh girls? Middle age. Something to look forward to, huh? Cycle of life. Remember that chart we made Lindy?

LINDY. Kind of. With the little arrows?

MRS B. Yep.

NORA. I liked that project.

MRS B. You're born, you learn to walk, you learn to talk, you go to school, you get really good grades, you get into a pretty good college, not great, not your first choice, but good. Lots of trees. A nice girls college. You do pretty well, not great…you're maybe not as smart as you hoped, but you're not dumb either. You're full of hope. You get a job. You fall in love, you get married, you have a kid. You're an adult. That little space between adult hood and old age…it's like fifty years… it's most of your life. And that tiny little space between those two arrows, that space is like a goddamn sea of fucking variables. That space…

> *(pause)*

Oh God.

> *(pause)*

My husband's having an affair.

*(**MRS BRAUGHMER** cries. The girls stand there not knowing what to do.)*

NORA. I've read that happens sometimes in middle age.

*(**MRS BRAUGHMER** takes a big sip of beer.)*

MRS B. So Lindy…how are things at home…with the flower shop and all?

LINDY. Fine.

MRS B. How's your mother?

LINDY. I guess she's okay. She kinda hasn't been around much. That's why we're out. I mean…she's not home.

MRS B. It's a funny thing this love business. It bites you hard sometimes.

LINDY. Yeah yeah. I know.

NORA. This has happened to a lot of powerful women Mrs. Braughmer. Think of Hilary Clinton.

LINDY. Yeah.

JENNY. I'm sorry Mrs. Braughmer but my ears are getting cold.

MRS B. So Lindy…where's your Dad?

LINDY. He's away on business.

MRS B. Hm.

(pause)

You scouts up for an adventure?

LINDY. Um…

MRS B. You know what sticks better than toilet paper?

LINDY/JENNY/NORA. Umm…

MRS B. Eggs. I got lots of eggs. The whites are like glue, and those yolks'll stick to the sides of the house and the screens and the windows. Shit. She won't get 'em off for months. Hold right there. I'll be back.

*(**MRS. BRAUGHMER** starts back into the house. She stops and looks back at the girls.)*

There should be a fucking badge for *this*.

> *(She rushes back into the house. The girls stand on the lawn clutching the toilet paper.)*

LINDY. What do we do?

NORA. This is weird.

JENNY. Mrs. Baughmer is like, wasted.

NORA. Technically she's probably just buzzed.

JENNY. She is totally wasted. She said fuck.

LINDY. Can you imagine if one of your parents were having an affair? That would be a nightmare.

JENNY. My Dad had an affair. That's why my Mom's rich.

LINDY. That makes me so sad. I feel sorry for her.

JENNY. Who? Mrs. Braughmer or my Mom?

LINDY. Duh. Mrs. Braughmer.

JENNY. It happens to a lot of families, Lindy. It could even happen to yours.

LINDY. Shut up Jenny. Just because your family has been through hard times doesn't mean my family…

NORA. You guys, stop. Mr. Baughmer wouldn't do that. He's a very nice man. He helps Lindy's mom with the flower shop every Thursday.

JENNY. Right.

> *(realization)*

Oh.

NORA. Maybe he's just working late to buy Jimmy a Prius.

JENNY. Nora, Jimmy isn't gonna drive for like, three years.

NORA. That's what I'm *saying*. These things take *time*.

LINDY. Poor Jimmy. He's gonna be so sad. Maybe I could write him a note. Or my Mom could send him a plant or something.

JENNY. Right. Lindy…we should go.

LINDY. What? No way. We have to do this.

JENNY. But um… Mrs. Braughmer is totally wasted…

NORA. Not technically.

JENNY. …and it's really late and maybe we should just let her do her thing.

LINDY. Mr. Braughmer is being an asshole.

JENNY. Yeah but, it's not really our business…and besides…

LINDY. Not our business? How can you say that? Don't you even care?

JENNY. I do but… I'm wearing bedroom slippers and I don't even know where we're going. I don't want my feet to get wet and end up catching a cold…

LINDY. Oh my God. What is like…your obsession with staying warm? It's so self involved.

JENNY. Oh my God. Self involved?

LINDY. Yeah. Self involved.

NORA. Lindy that's not nice.

LINDY. I don't care.

JENNY. Lindy do you have any idea what's going on?

LINDY. Yeah.

JENNY. Oh. Well…

LINDY. You don't love Jimmy. You never did.

JENNY. What?

LINDY. So stop saying you do when its obvious you don't. And I'm sorry to bring it out in the open, but its time you like…faced facts. Jimmy likes me better and you know it.

JENNY. Oh my God.

NORA. Guys, let's take a deep breath and…

LINDY. I know he likes me. He like looks at me in history all the time. And he sent me a note saying he liked my hair and I feel like I can't tell you about it cause you'll get mad but it's true. I'm sick of pretending this isn't happening when it's happening. My life is changing. And you can't come with me.

JENNY. What?

LINDY. Cause like, what's gonna happen when Jimmy asks me to Spring Fling? Are you gonna go with Nicholas?

I don't think so. Cause Nicholas is going with Jasmine and…

JENNY. Jimmy asked you to Spring Fling?

NORA. Guys…

LINDY. Not yet, but he's gonna. I can tell.

NORA. You guys listen…

JENNY. Jesus Lindy. I hate to break it to you…but he didn't mention that he liked you when he sent me a note saying he liked my hair *and* making a joke about politics. You live in a dream world Lindy. Jimmy barely knows who you are!

(**LINDY** *charges at* **JENNY**. *Girlfight.*)

LINDY. That is not true! Take it back.

JENNY. Okay. Okay you want a piece of me? FINE. Just FINE!

NORA. You guys stop. We're gonna get in trouble. THIS IS A NIGHTMARE!

(**MRS. B** *is heard singing at the doorway holding a bottle of scotch, a bag of sweaters and a carton of eggs.*)

MRS B. *"Bye bye Mrs. American pie. Drove my Chevy to the levee but the levee was dry…"*

(**LINDY** *and* **JENNY** *stop fighting. They are crying, out of breath.*)

"And good ol' boys drinkin whiskey and rye singin…"

NEIGHBOR. (*offstage*) WHAT IS GOING ON OUT THERE?

MRS B. MIND YOUR OWN BUSINESS MRS. BARKER! AND IF YOU PUT ONE MORE RELIGIOUS PAMPHLET ON MY DOORSTEP I WILL TELL THE PTA COMMITTEE YOU STOLE MY RECIPE FOR CHOCOLATE SANDIES YOU PASSIVE AGGRESSIVE BITCH!

(*sound of window shutting abruptly*)

Huh. I've been waiting to do that for ten years.

(*She drinks.*)

Best fucking chocolate sandies. FUCK YOU you thief! Thieves! These WOMEN. That's why *we* have to stick together girls. We have to…be there for one another. We have to be girls' girls. True blue. Friendship. Real fucking female friendship. Girl Scout law. Okay. I got eggs. Lookie here. Three eggs each. That way, we can hit the house from all angles, see? And I brought sweaters and hats so we don't catch cold.

(She pulls out a sweater.)

Here, this one's Jimmy's. You'll have to fight over it.

(NORA takes the sweater.)

NORA. I'll take it.

LINDY. No! Its mine!

JENNY. Nora!

NORA. What?

(JENNY grabs the sweater roughly.)

JENNY. Got it.

LINDY. Jenny! Be careful. It's his SWEATER. You don't even care.

NORA. Can I touch it?

MRS B. Can you touch it? Touch it girls. Go ahead. It's a sweater. Made from a lamb. They shave it off. Doesn't hurt the lamb. No sir. The lamb is fine. Just a little chilly. A little cut up. Ooh! Nora! Hat!

NORA. Oh. Oh!

(MRS. BAUGHMER throws NORA a 49ers cap.)

MRS B. The 49ers. I hate football. And Lindy…

(MRS. BAUGHMER throws LINDY a leather jacket.)

LINDY. Oh my God.

MRS B. Leather jacket. "My boy needs a leather jacket."

JENNY. He wore that to the dance.

MRS B. Why didn't ya ever give me a leather jacket you goddamn son-of-a-bitch?

LINDY. It smells like him.

MRS B. Ugh.

JENNY. No fair. He wore that when he danced with *me*.

LINDY. *No Jenny you have his sweater!*

NORA. His head's been in this hat!

MRS B. Girls enough! Jenny, be a giver not a taker. You always had a problem with that. Always hoarding those thin mints. Here, take this hat.

JENNY. THAT'S NOT FAIR! I wasn't hoarding them. My Dad loves thin mints. I was just trying to… I'm not a taker. I'm not trying to hurt you Lindy! God. Fine! Do what you want. I'm going home.

LINDY. Oh yeah right. You don't care. You just wanna run off when the going gets tough. You want to steal his sweater so you can run home and curl up in it. You won't even wear it. Just like that dog you begged for that you never even walk.

JENNY. What?

LINDY. You just wanted to *have* her.

NORA. Lindy that's…

JENNY. I'm allergic. It's not my fault.

LINDY. It doesn't matter. You should get some medicine. You should tough it out.

> (**NORA**, *frustrated with being ignored, pulls a book and a flashlight out of her bag and starts to read.*)

JENNY. But…

LINDY. You don't deserve Jimmy. I love him more. He's mine. You don't know how to care for anything. *You don't know how to love.*

JENNY. Oh yeah?

LINDY. YEAH.

MRS B. GIRLS!

JENNY. All right. Fine! Go ahead and egg your own house. If you think that will make Jimmy like you…fine!

MRS B. ENOUGH!

LINDY. What are you talking about?

(JENNY *takes off the sweater and starts to leave.*)

JENNY. You're such an idiot. Here…take the sweater, I don't care. I'll freeze to death. Fine.

LINDY. Jenny…wait…

JENNY. Ask Mrs. Braughmer whose house we're egging.

MRS B. Oh no you don't Jenny. You didn't have a problem messin' with my house for your little love situation so you better believe you're coming with me.

JENNY. Go ahead. You're so tough. Ask her who's house it is. I DARE YOU.

(*pause*)

LINDY. Whose house are we egging Mrs. B?

MRS B. Jenny you little…always poking your nose…

LINDY. Whose house are we egging?

(*pause*)

MRS B. Goddammit.

(**MRS. BRAUGHMER** *sits down and takes a swig of scotch.*)

LINDY. You haven't answered the question Mrs. Braughmer.

(**MRS. BRAUGHMER** *takes another swig.*)

MRS B. Poor lamb. So innocent. Standing there with your big Bambi eyes and your flat little chest.

JENNY. Mrs. Braughmer, that's not very nice

MRS B. Nice? You want me to be nice? You want me to be… Huh.

LINDY. Why doesn't someone just tell me what's going on?

MRS B. I just wanted to hear 'em crack as they slid down the wall. For once in my life… I just wanted to throw something hard.

JENNY. We're going to egg *your* house Lindy. Duh.

LINDY. What? But why? Nobody's even home.

MRS B. Well Lindy…where do you think she is?

LINDY. Oh God. Oh no.

JENNY. I was trying to tell you.

LINDY. Oh my God.

MRS B. Sorry to break it to you kid. Life's a peach.

LINDY. But…

MRS B. Why do ya think your mom's gone every Saturday night and Sunday day, huh?

LINDY. She's just…she's takes singing class in the bay area on Saturday. Spends the night at her friend Debbie's to beat the traffic. That's why…

MRS B. Huh.

NORA. Some men find singing very sexy.

MRS B. Do you ever hear her sing honey?

NORA. I'm still not clear about what's going on.

MRS B. Nora, Mr. Braughmer is having an affair with Mrs. Kramer.

LINDY. Oh my God.

NORA. What? Really? But that doesn't make any sense. Lindy's mom is so nice.

(**LINDY** *starts to cry.* **JENNY** *hugs her.*)

LINDY. Why? Why would she do that to Dad? Why? She's such a bitch.

JENNY. It's all gonna be okay. I swear to you. Your parents are gonna feel guilty…they're gonna be so nice to you…you're gonna get so much stuff. I bet you go to Disneyland. I bet you go…

MRS B. I don't know Lindy. I can't figure it out. Your mother and I, I like her. I thought we were friends.

(*She drinks.*)

How could I kiss him goodbye every morning and not notice a difference? I just didn't think Walter would ever… I mean, maybe if he had been a little more… I would have responded. Maybe I shoulda opened the door wrapped in fucking Saran Wrap or vacuumed in my bra like that fucking book my mother gave me. It just always seemed so inconvenient and not really sexy. I mean…do ya wrap your legs *together* or one at a time? Shit. I can barely put Saran Wrap over a bowl…let alone over my…

LINDY. Why are you telling us this?

JENNY. Lindy…

LINDY. This is disgusting! Aren't you supposed to be setting an example? Our Girl Scout troop sucked. We only sold 36 boxes of cookies. You like…never even knew how to tie a knot.

JENNY. Lindy…

LINDY. No. We hated you. Didn't we? Didn't we? SAY IT.

NORA. Not really she taught us a lot.

LINDY. Fine. Fine. *I* hated you.

MRS B. Really?

LINDY. Yeah.

MRS B. Huh.

(pause)

I mean…that's what you get when you go sneaking around at two in the morning throwing toilet paper on people's roses. I mean, if you're gonna put yourself out there like that, you have to be prepared.

NORA. You taught us that in Scouts.

MRS B. Yep.

NORA. I was always confused about what exactly we needed to be prepared *for*. I mean, besides overnight camping trips at the Y.

LINDY. You wanted me to egg my own house?

MRS B. Yeah. I guess so.

(pause)

LINDY. That sucks.

JENNY. I was trying to tell you.

MRS B. You know what? It's good you said that. Cause it does suck. It's good. Let it out. You know what? Let's all let it out. Let's all chomp on a big truth sandwich huh? I'm calling an official meeting. The subject of our meeting is: let's fucking say how we really feel. Jenny, you go first.

(The girls sit in a circle like they did when they were scouts.)

JENNY. Um…

MRS B. Go. Let'er rip.

JENNY. Um… Lindy… I feel like, since we both started liking Jimmy we're not even friends anymore. 'Cause you have thing where you think you love Jimmy the most no matter what I say and it's like…now there's this like competition between us. Like when Jimmy gave me that muffin…

LINDY. Jimmy gave you a muffin?

NORA. Guys…

JENNY. Yeah. 'Cause it's like…if I say one word about Jimmy like…there's this whole part of my day I don't even tell you about. 'Cause I know you'll freak out, and like judge me. And it's really too bad cause I used to like talking on the phone with you more than anything.

LINDY. Me too.

NORA. Guys…

LINDY. I'm so sorry I said that about the sweater. About you taking things and being self involved.

MRS B. Oh yeah. Sometimes I put on Walter's ties, and I sit in the bath.

NORA. Guys…

LINDY. 'Cause…like… I don't know what its like to have divorced parents. And I know I never really talked to you about your parents…

JENNY. Yeah…

MRS B. Just sit in that bath and let the water soak all the way up. Never knew why I did. Hid it. Like a compulsion.

NORA. Actually I've been meaning…

JENNY. That thing I said about Jimmy not knowing who you are was a lie…

NORA. Umm…

JENNY. I know Jimmy knows who you are. He…he thinks you're really pretty.

LINDY. Really?

JENNY. Yeah. I should have told you that, like, last week. I'm sorry.

NORA. So, um…

LINDY. You're my best friend Jenny.

JENNY. You're my best friend too.

    (**JENNY** and **LINDY** hug.)

NORA. Jimmy kissed me.

JENNY & LINDY. What?

MRS B. Jesus Christ.

NORA. He kissed me. Right on the lips. Last Wednesday. Right after gym class. I wanted to tell you guys…but… I was so confused 'cause…and I didn't know how. 'Cause you guys have been my best friends for two years now, and I don't wanna mess that up. He said, Nora… I like you 'cause you're quiet and smart and then he kissed me. And… I didn't feel anything. Nothing at all. Just lips. Like, I could have been kissing a sausage. I wish… I wish… I could feel things like you guys, but I don't. I've just been like, pretending to like him so you know…we could all be together. And I'm finding it really exhausting. And all of this boy girl stuff is really freaking me out. I hate it. I really hate it.

I really wish things could go back to how they used to be, you know like in elementary school when we all just got along and we could be friends with boys too.

    (pause.)

And… Jimmy asked me to the Spring Fling, okay? But don't worry, cause I said no cause I'm not that interested so he still might ask one of you.

MRS B. Huh. And here we are girls. And here...we...are.

(**MRS. BRAUGHMER** *takes two eggs out of the carton. She hands one to* **LINDY**.)

Here ya go.

(**MRS. BRAUGHMER** *throws the other egg against the front door.*)

Take that you son of a bitch. HA! Go ahead Lindy.

(**LINDY** *is hesitant.*)

Just go ahead. Throw it hard, from your whole arm.

LINDY. But...

MRS B. THROW IT FOR CHRISSAKES.

LINDY. Yes Mrs. Braughmer.

ASSHOLE.

(**LINDY** *throws it. The egg hits the window and smears down.*)

MRS B. Did that help?

LINDY. Yes.

JENNY. You'll never get that out. It'll drip down the pane. And then it sticks.

(*Pause. They all stare at the dripping eggs.*)

MRS B. Hey...you girls want some breakfast? I got all these eggs. We could make an omelette. Mix in a little cheese and onion.

LINDY. Okay.

NORA. Sure.

JENNY. I'm so hungry I could eat a horse.

NORA. That's disgusting.

LINDY. It's just an expression.

(**MRS BRAUGHMER** *surveys the mess.*)

MRS B. Nah, let him clean it up.

(*The girls file in.* **LINDY** *is last. She takes the "We love Jimmy" sign and breaks it in half before* *entering the house.* **MRS B** *takes a final look down the driveway.*)

I need to talk to that boy.

CPSIA information can be obtained
at www.ICGtesting.com
Printed in the USA
LVHW060141180723
752622LV00065B/1212

9 780573 704802